STORAGE STORIES

Jim Bob

STORAGE STORIES

First published in 2010 by Ten Forty Books
PO Box 709 London SE19 1JY

Cover design: John Facundo

Printed in the UK by CPI Mackays, Chatham, ME5 8TD

A catalogue record for this book is available from The British Library

ISBN: 978-0-9564049-0-9

www.storagestories.co.uk
www.tenfortybooks.com

STORAGE STORIES

"You can't have everything. Where would you put it?" –
Steven Wright.

WHERE ARE THEY NOW?

I was being interviewed for a music magazine. And like the old joke about lawyers, I could tell the journalist was lying, because his lips were moving.

"It's not *where are they now?*" he said. "It's more *where* they *are* now. It's rhetorical, there's no question mark. It isn't one of those has-been round-ups like in other magazines. This won't be a bitchy article about how you're not so famous any more. What we really like to do is let our readers know where you're at, what you've been up to, if you've got anything new you want to promote."

The background noise at the other end of the phone line changed. And I knew the journalist was cupping his hand over the receiver. I knew his shoulders were shaking with suppressed laughter, like Edward Heath's used to do. A small damp patch would be darkening the front of his trousers as the music journalist actually started to piss himself.

I knew he was desperate for the interview to end so he could hang up the phone and snort and guffaw and laugh his head off. He wanted to join in with all the other music journalists gathered around his desk in their chant of *Haasbeeen, Haasbeeen* before throwing another dart into a picture of me that was pinned to the office dartboard.

"Think of the piece as a map on a bus shelter. One of those maps with a big arrow that says *you are here*." He said.

What a fucking liar.

Three months later there I was on page five of the magazine, under the heading *Where Are They Now?* There was a big question mark at the centre of my forehead, in the most acne-splattered and pasty picture of me that was ever taken. The same picture they'd been chucking darts at twelve weeks earlier.

On the page with me there were some other has-beens who'd dropped off the rock radar and been picked up by the ridicule one. Where were they now? The magazine asked. How far and hard had they fallen? How loud should we be laughing? How wet should our trousers be? Next to my spotty picture there was a photograph of a female singer who was once referred to as the English Madonna. She was pictured selling copies of her own album from behind the counter of the pound shop where she now worked. That, as they say,. is show business.

The magazine sneered and scoffed at how *yesterday* we all were and how all the time they'd been bigging us up in the past – giving our records ten out of tens and putting our faces on the front cover - all that time they'd actually thought we were, in fact, shit.

There was nothing in the write-up beneath my picture about how I was now working as a solo artist, still making music, working on a new album. None of the stuff I'd told the journalist about my new musical direction and maturity, and how I had no regrets but still many unfulfilled ambitions.

No mention of my planned tour of pubs and clubs and how I was looking forward to playing some sweaty, intimate gigs again. Seeing the whites of the audience's eyes like in the good old days before I'd become so annoyingly successful and popular. Nothing about how I wanted to get in the back of a crappy van and just have a laugh again.

Like the journalist, I'd lied too.

I should have told him that, rather than working on a new album, I hadn't actually written a song for ages. The hard skin on my fingertips from playing the guitar had softened and I hadn't had a microphone-related cold sore for almost a year. I didn't tell him about the day I'd faced up to every former pop star's nightmare, the most terrifying prospect of all.

I might have to get a proper job.

Maybe I should have just faxed him a copy of this newspaper ad:

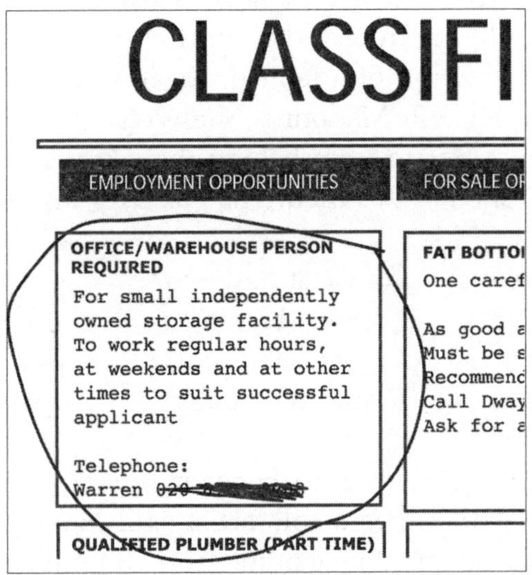

CLASSIFI

EMPLOYMENT OPPORTUNITIES

OFFICE/WAREHOUSE PERSON REQUIRED

For small independently owned storage facility. To work regular hours, at weekends and at other times to suit successful applicant

Telephone:
Warren 020-[illegible]

QUALIFIED PLUMBER (PART TIME)

FOR SALE OF

FAT BOTTO

One caref

As good a
Must be s
Recommend
Call Dway
Ask for a

That's where I was now.

STORAGE STORIES

CARL

Here's a picture of our company van:

It's the one that Carl used to drive before he was taken away in a different van. That van looked something like this:

JANIE

This is Janie who works part time in the office. Janie looks like the French actress Juliette Binoche.

Sometimes Janie comes in to work with a black eye.

Or wearing a sticky plaster.

HAL

This is HAL. Named after the computer in *2001: A Space Odyssey*. HAL is our very own homicidal computer.

MICHAEL STIPE

This is Michael Stipe from REM. Not the same Michael Stipe who stores his worn-out arcade machines with us. Just a coincidence.

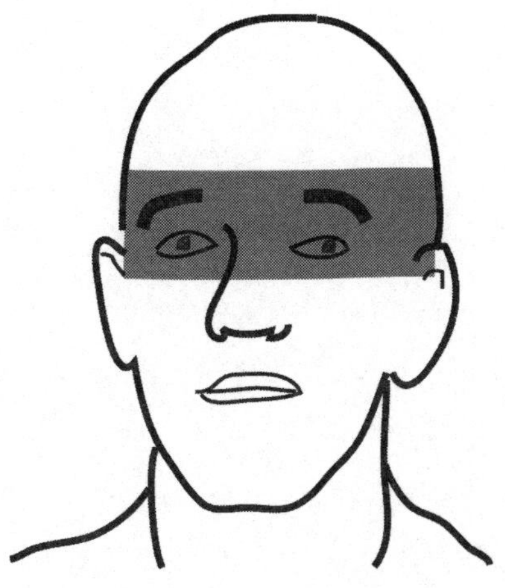

This is the most miserable sweetshop in the world. It's where we buy our milk and newspapers.

And this is me.

Before I was famous, when nobody knew or cared where I was now, I rented fifty square feet of storage space to store the contents of my parents' home after they both passed away. The deaths of both my parents were equally sudden, tragic and heart-related. Although I suppose if you think about it, all deaths are heart-related and more often than not tragic and sudden.

I had to sort through my mum and dad's cupboards and drawers, something I hadn't done since I was a schoolboy looking for cigarettes, small change or alcohol. I had to sift through all their fading photographs, receipts, utility bills, personal letters and all the bits and pieces they'd accumulated during their combined time on Earth. I found photograph albums and packets of photos that hadn't made it into albums.

Pictures of my mum almost falling out of shot and focus, doubled up in fits of hysterical laughter brought on by other photos of my dad in one of his plastic Groucho Marx masks or his joke shop tits, hunched up in the middle of his infamous Quasimodo impression. *The bells, Esmeralda, the bells,* Dad had written underneath one of the photographs.

There were holiday pictures that I'd taken. Photos of my mum, my dad and my sister Robin: eating 99s on a windy pier, with Dad doing rabbit's ears with his fingers behind Mum's head. There was a photograph of Dad chasing Mum into the salty wind and towards the pier's edge, pretending he was going to push her over into the sea below. The memories made me smile and at the same time made me feel like crying my eyes out.

I had to cut through gnarled old parcel tape and itchy string to open dusty brown leather suitcases from the top of the wardrobe and from under my parents' big empty bed. I sat on the bed with one big open case, the bedsprings creaking beneath our combined weight, and I thought about how my parents might have conceived me in this very bed. That too made me smile and at the same time feel like crying my eyes out. In one old brown suitcase I found three pairs of flip-flops and two holiday postcards with nothing written on. The front of one postcard was completely black apart from the words *Littlehampton At Night* and the other postcard had a cartoon picture of a couple in deckchairs on a beach drinking tea. Behind the cartoon couple was a camel and beneath the picture it said *One Hump Or Two?* In the same suitcase there were two whoopee cushions, a set of chattering teeth, a box of pretend chocolates, a rubber chicken and what I thought was a can of mixed nuts until I opened it and a paper snake sprang out almost causing the third sudden, heart related family death that month.

I sorted my parents' belongings into various piles, cardboard boxes, black bin bags and supermarket carriers. I labelled everything with old luggage tags I found in a desk drawer.

I went through my parents' wardrobe which was packed tight with suits and dresses, some still wrapped in cellophane from the dry cleaners. There was a pale green paper label pinned to the cuff of my dad's black pin-striped three-piece – cleaned and pressed, ready and waiting for the next wedding or funeral. What did he wear to his own funeral? The smell of my parents' clothes made me think of an Oxfam shop or a Scope, or a church hall on jumble sale day.

There was a rack of my father's novelty ties hanging on a rail on the inside of the wardrobe door. Novelty ties with cartoon characters and pictures of fruit and fish – *kipper tie,* one said – it was shaped like a fish and if you so desired, you could fill it with water and squirt it at someone for a laugh. Many of the ties were wide, as wide as an Osmond Brother's smile. There were also a dozen bow ties, two of which were battery powered. I flicked the switch on the back of one of the bow ties and watched it draw one last lame spin from the old batteries. I unhooked the rack of big fat daft and loud ties from the wardrobe door and stuffed them into a black rubbish sack, such a lot of zany neckties. If I'd knotted them together I could have climbed out of my parents' second floor bedroom window and escaped all the sadness.

I took some of my parents' belongings to a charity shop and some of it I threw away. Everything else went into storage.

You can tell a lot about people from their storage. Mum and Dad had kept everything. There were three different zoo guidebooks: one with a gorilla on the front cover, one with a giraffe and the other with a painting of a zebra and a monkey.

I'd once asked my dad about the time he first met my mother. He told me it was on a clammy day at London Zoo in 1969.

"It was so hot that day that I wouldn't have been surprised to hear that the zebras' stripes had peeled off in the heat and there was now a brand new breed of white horse in their enclosure." My dad said.

He first saw my mother standing by the penguin pool, laughing at the penguins tripping over each other and sliding into the water.

"Have you ever wondered what penguins wear when they aren't on their way to a posh dinner and dance?" he'd said to her, no doubt making the sound and doing the mime of somebody playing a short drum roll and cymbal crash. "Do you think if we stand here long enough those zookeepers will throw us some fish too? I'm starving."

Mum had said the first time she remembered seeing my dad wasn't at the penguin pool but when she'd noticed him making faces at some kids who were teasing the gorillas.

"I'd made some remark to your dad about the kids being cheeky monkeys. And he said that *technically* the gorilla is an ape. I told him that of course I meant the kids, *they* were the cheeky monkeys. There was no stopping him then. He said that technically, the species in question was the cheeky sod."

After that my mother had gone off to watch a python eat a dead mouse while Dad had a date with an elephant and a bag of doughnuts, or duffnuts as he always liked to call them. He also called biscuits 'biskwits'.

Mum and Dad both loved London Zoo. Mum particularly liked the polar bears while Dad liked the penguins and the elephants. Once, when he went along to feed duffnuts to his favourite elephant Dixie and found poor Dixie had recently fallen into the moat surrounding the elephant house and died, he said he thought his heart had broken. He said the zoo was the only fun place his own Father had ever taken him when he was a boy and he thought that if he ever had a son himself, he'd take him there all the time. And he lived up to his promise. Once a year, usually on the hottest day, Dad would take me to the zoo, right up until I was nineteen, when he said that we looked more like a gay couple on a date than father and son.

Later on that hot day, the day they first met, my mum and dad had both caught the same packed zoo bus back to Baker Street Underground station.

"I asked your dad if he was following me," Mum told me. "And he said, yes, he was a spy, that's why he was wearing sneakers. He was wearing sandals. Heavy buckled brown leather sandals that squeaked with the bus brakes when it turned a corner or stopped at traffic lights. And even though it was so incredibly hot he wore them with thick woolly socks."

Those sandals were at the back of the wardrobe, between a pair of yachting shoes, some Wellington boots with a comedy L in white insulation tape on the right one and an R peeling off the left. I put the sandals, yachting shoes and Wellingtons in a black bag with all my parents' other shoes. A lot of my father's footwear looked as though it had been prescribed by a chiropodist rather than bought from a shoe shop. The rest of his wardrobe was knitted and woven in a laboratory. If he was wearing one of his many Bri-Nylon shirts on that clammy day in Regents Park, it would have been stuck fast to his back with static electricity and perspiration.

"I remember your dad was wearing all these badges. *DANGEROUS ANIMAL DO NOT FEED* and something about Twiggy and mini skirts."

FORGET OXFAM FEED TWIGGY and *UP WITH MINI*

SKIRTS. I found all three badges in a shoebox under the bed. I put them in a cardboard box.

Flower power, the Beatles and the Stones had little effect on my dad. Just a few novelty badges on a man made shirt. Mum, on the other hand, would have looked like the Chelsea Flower Show. In those old seaside photos she always wore some home-sewn dandelion-and-daisy patterned trouser suit or full-body culottes, the flared legs flowing majestically to the floor, like the curtains in her bedroom.

Mum had finished the story of how she'd met my dad. Telling me how on the zoo bus Dad had told her polar bear jokes all the way to Baker Street tube station. I'd heard them myself plenty of times since.

"And do you know why polar bears have fur coats?" Dad would have asked.

"No, why?" My unsuspecting mother would have replied.

"Because they'd freeze to death in Hawaiian shirts!"

"Why shouldn't you take polar bears to the zoo?"

"I don't know, why shouldn't you take polar bears to the zoo?"

"Because they'd rather go to the pictures."

"What did the polar bear eat after the dentist fixed its tooth?"

"I don't know."

"The dentist."

He would have had my mother laughing all the way to Baker Street station.

"What do you get when you cross a polar bear with a seal?"

"A polar bear."

"What's white, furry, and plays cricket?"

"A bowler bear!"

"What's white, furry, wears sunglasses and lies in the sun?"

"A solar bear!"

" What's white, furry, smokes cigars, and stays up all night playing cards?"

" A poker bear!"

"When is a polar bear not a polar bear?"

"When it's in a grizzly mood."

"How do you get a polar bear into a fridge?"

"Open the door, polar bears like cold places."

And all the way to Clapham Common on the Underground.

"We were married within a year." Mum said.

It's a well-known family legend how at the wedding ceremony Dad had jokingly agreed to take Mum to be his *awful wedded wife* and how at the reception he placed a whoopee cushion on her chair. He made a speech that was something like *I'd like to thanooooaaarrrgghhhoowwww* as he pretended to faint face first into the cake. Another family legend tells of how in the function room's toilets, Dad had waited for fifteen minutes in one of the cubicles for his new father-in-law to come in, so Dad could drop a marble into the toilet bowl and say, "Oh no, my glass eye!"

I know that when they honeymooned in Littlehampton Dad would have chased Mum up the stairs of their honeymoon hotel, making her scream like a six-year old girl.

"I kneeeed you," he'd tell her as he leant his knee into the side of her leg. "I've got a crush on you," he'd say, squashing his newlywed wife into the wall. And his all-time favourite, "Am I *getting on your nerves?*" as he pushed his knuckles into Mum's side. He did it to my mother. He did it to me. And he did it to my sister Robin.

I was the first child. Born on April Fools Day, two years before my sister Robin - *the Girl Wonder*. I'd soon grow to dread my birthday. Why couldn't my mother have held on a day longer, kept her legs crossed for just 24 more hours? Every year Dad would pretend he'd forgotten my birthday again. Right up until after noon, when the day of practical joking was officially over and he could finally bring my presents out of hiding. Presents that would frequently include some fake dogshit, a plastic spider or a tiny empty box wrapped up in yards and yards of wrapping paper.

Birthday breakfast would be a plate of rubber bacon and eggs or a blue mouth sweet or stick of cardboard chewing gum on a spring that would almost snap my finger off when I took it from my wise-cracking father. Then I'd get to spend the rest of the day trying to blow out the novelty candles on my birthday cake, Dad laughing till he cried as they went out and reignited over and over. When I reached my teens I tried staying awake as late as possible the night before my birthday, in the hope that I'd be so tired that I wouldn't wake until the foolproof safety of the afternoon. The second year that I tried this, I awoke at midday to find that my dad had sneaked into my room in the middle of the night and sewn my bed sheets together.

And that was just April. Dad also celebrated January, February and March Fools Day. May, June and July Fools Day, August, September, October, November and December Fools Day. And then he'd start all over again, preceding every new January Fools Day by kissing us all goodnight on December the 31st and saying, "See you all next year", before chasing Mum upstairs as she screamed like a Blue Peter presenter. I'd hear them from the room next door, Dad in bed beside Mum, poking her lovingly in the back of the neck with his knuckles and asking if he was getting on her nerves.

My sister and me moved away from our parents around the same time as each other. Robin married to escape the madhouse – Dad repeating the same comic speech from his own wedding, face first into another complicated three-storey cake. I left home to become a mature student in a university at the other end of the country and plan my musical career.

"Mature student? There's an oxymoron if ever I heard one," my father had joked, and he then went on to list all the oxymorons he could think of: Baby giant. Clean toilet. Casual sex. Dry martini. Live television. Marital bliss. Light heavyweight. Fresh yogurt. Etc etc.

With Robin and me gone, Mum and Dad began their second childhood.

It was all there in the storage. Till receipts, almost faded back to blank. Ticket stubs and tiny pens and pencils, stolen from DIY stores.

Every Sunday after Robin and me were gone, my parents would drive out to B & Q or to Ikea, where they'd laugh at the comical Swedish furniture names. They bought a wall shelf because it was called Robin like their daughter and a bookshelf named after me.

Mum and Dad would sometimes skip the furniture displays and go straight to the big and cheap Scandinavian Ikea restaurant to share a plate of meatballs, Dad pointing at imaginary meatball gravy on Mum's blouse like he loved to do, and then gently flicking the end of her nose with his finger when she looked down. She fell for it every time. Every single time.

The university graduates and resting actors in their brightly coloured tabards, collecting bank details for charity in the High Street, fell for Dad's tricks too. When he was walking down the street towards one of them, Dad would wait until just before they pounced on him. And then a split second before they asked him whether he could spare just a few moments of his time, he'd shout *Boo!* making them jump out of their brightly coloured tabards, leaving Dad to carry on down the High Street whistling and chuckling to himself.

In the summer months my parents would drive out to a country pub and sit in the beer garden with their pub lunches. Dad would have a mixed grill and Mum the surf & turf. £2.66 and £2.40 respectively (they'd kept the receipts). They'd sit outside and watch the kids on the slides and swings, like they used to do with Robin and me, waiting for the pub playground to empty so they could have a go. Dad would push Mum higher and higher on the swing until she screamed.

"Stop, you bugger, *STOOOOOOPPP!*"

At the end of the day he'd chase her up the stairs to bed and she'd scream as he puffed and wheezed behind her, his man boobs bobbing up and down.

"Stop it, I'll wet myself. Stoooooopppp you old bugger! *Stoooopppppp!*"

Towards the end of my mother's eighteen-month wait for a hospital bed and a new hip, when she had to use a wheelchair to get about, Dad would wheel her to the cinema during the day when it was empty. They'd watch Disney movies alone together in the dark and snuggle up in front of feel good rom-coms. They'd share stupidly deep tubs of popcorn and buckets of watered down Pepsi and Dad would always blow the wrapper from his drinking straw into Mum's face, making her laugh louder and feel more good than any of the films ever could. After the movie he'd wheel his wife to Burger King or McDonalds and order a kids' meal so he could annoy the person serving them and get the free toy or colouring book.

I put the plastic cartoon characters into the box with the badges and torn cinema tickets.

On the way back home from the cinema Dad would keep letting go of the wheelchair at the top of a hill.

"I've got you!" he'd say and "Oh, no I haven't!" and again, "It's okay I've…got…no I haven't… *woooaahh*… oh yes I have."

And Mum would scream with hysterical laughter again. On the back of the wheelchair my dad had taped a learner driver L-plate and hung a pair of furry dice from the handles.

Both in a box, destined for storage.

While Mum was in hospital my father would have provided the doctors and nurses with more entertainment than a posse of hospital DJs. He'd bookmarked one of his joke books at the *Hospital and Medical Funnies* section.

"My wife's got some vinegar in her ear, Doctor," he'd say. "Do you think she might be suffering from pickled hearing?" And "Nurse, I think my wife has swallowed her pillow, she's feeling a little down in the mouth." Stuff like that. He must have had the other patients in stitches (© page 32). His favourite medical joke was, "Do you see the red pen the doctor has in his top pocket? That's so he can draw blood." They say that laughter is the best medicine.

Two days before Mum was discharged from hospital my dad managed to get the BBC's *Ground Force* team to makeover their front garden. I came home for that. Mum said over and over again how she was speechless when she saw the new garden and she cried as she drank her glass of champagne with Charlie, Tommy and the rest of the team in her brand new almost-finished gazebo. Dad was lucky that Tommy hadn't hit him with his shovel when he'd put his hand out to shake Dad's and Dad had lifted it, put his thumb on the end of his nose and waggled his fingers at the large TV gardener as though he were playing an invisible trumpet. And as for all his cold weather jokes with Charlie Dimmock that never made it into the final programme…

When I'd visited Mum in prison she'd told me how when her new hip had settled into its place at the top of her leg, Dad had booked a two-week holiday for the two of them in Spain. On the flight there he had constantly called the stewardess nurse and asked her to hold his dentures for him "for just a moment please, nurse." Once the plane was high up above the clouds Dad pushed his seat back, clasped his hands behind his head and said in a loud voice, "Thank God for auto-pilot, it's so good to get a bit of time away from the cockpit to sleep my hangover off."

When they arrived in Spain, Mum and Dad would spend whole days on the beach laughing. Dad would take my mother by the hand down to the water's edge and lead her into the sea, where he'd gently splash her till she laughed and screamed and then he'd hold his nose and he'd say, "Down periscope!" and sink under the water. Back on the beach he'd pass a large seashell to the couple sitting next to them. "It's for you," he'd say, pretending it was a telephone.

At their holiday hotel my mother was still too unsure on her new hip to run up the stairs with her husband chasing her and making her scream like a six-year old girl or a Blue Peter presenter, so they'd take the lift instead. Dad would press every button on the way up to their eleventh floor room, stopping at each level to say stuff like, "First floor, ladies underwear, haberdashery, moustache trimmings and fine wines. Second floor: wigs, large inflatables, lesbianism and piano tuning." And so on.

On the flight home to England Dad had leant across to the passenger sitting opposite and said that he was glad to see the pilot was doing so well since he last saw him at the Alcoholics Anonymous meeting… three days ago. At passport control he wore a Groucho Marx mask and received a telling off from a customs officer.

About a year later Mum was at home in the kitchen making some sandwiches for a Sunday afternoon picnic. My parents were going to drive out to Boxhill and eat their sandwiches under one of the Box trees as they looked out at Leith Hill and the South Downs. Dad was fidgety and impatient as usual and he kept pinching Mum's backside, pulling her love handles and pushing against her with his knee.

"I kneeeed you," he said. And "I've got a crush on you!" and he leant into his sandwich-making wife, cracking his favourite joke of all as he pushed his knuckles into the back of her neck. "Am I *getting on your nerves?"*

And my mother spun round.

"YES YOU ARE!" she screamed, and plunged the bread knife straight into her husband's heart – which couldn't have been easy, what with Dad's man boobs, Mum's arthritis and the bread knife's bevelled edge.

Eventually the police came. They drew a chalk outline around my dad and took my mum away in a police car. Perhaps it looked like this:

While she was awaiting trial, my mother passed away in her sleep. Everyone said she died of a broken heart, but they always say that, don't they.

THIS IS WARREN

Warren was the buck-toothed, jug-eared and baby-faced manager who interviewed me for my new job. When he asked me if I had any storage experience, I decided not to tell him about my mum and dad.

Warren said the storage world had had some bad press. I didn't tell him how yes, I understand, so had I. Warren said he presumed I'd read in the newspapers about record-breaking drugs seizures and tea chests full of illegal porn. I had. He presumed I'd heard recently about the murderer who kept his victims in self-storage. I had. I'd seen the blurry CCTV footage on the news. I'd watched the man offloading soggy black rubbish bags of blood and body parts in the middle of the night. Folding his dead wife into a chest freezer.

Warren asked me if I'd read about two brothers who stockpiled almost a ton of fertiliser in a storage warehouse near Luton Airport. I told him I had. The police said the men were going to use the fertiliser to make a big bomb. The men said they had a lot of gardening to do. I'd also heard how the police found such a vast amount of marijuana and skunk in one particular storage unit, that if there had been a fire, the whole town would have got the munchies.

"That's the trouble with some people," Warren said. "You provide them with a service and they take the piss."

Warren said that I'd find the contents of most people's storage space weren't anything I'd read about in the newspapers or see on the Nine O'clock News. He said it was mostly household and business overspill. Students out of the country on extended holidays and gap years. Newlyweds and divorcees. Rock bands and bankrupt shopkeepers.

"Hoarders and collectors, hamsters and squirrelers," Warren said. "Junk-ies and space cadets. Men from Mars and women from Venus. Your life is a thousand piece jigsaw puzzle and you've got fifteen hundred pieces," Warren said. "Who you gonna call?"

I laughed. I got the joke. *Ghostbusters* right? Warren said he liked me and he gave me the job.

For six months I answered the phone, swept up, gave people keys and padlocks and chased rats and unpaid rental bills. I forgot about my solo album and my planned tour of pubs and clubs and became more involved in the day-to-day running of the place. I read the storage trade magazines that were delivered every month. And not just to draw moustaches on the pictures of some of the weirdoes who worked in the industry like I did when I first started working here.

In one of the magazines I read an interview with American storage big Mac and cheese Jack J Renumba, the billionaire boss of Big Storage Inc U.S.A. Jack J had this to say about the future of the UK storage industry.

"London has density. 5 million people squeezed into just a few hundred square miles of space. All those small houses and small businesses tightly packed together in such close proximity. Londoners need more space. Estimates show that self-storage spaces per capita in London are less than 5 percent of what they are in the United States. To reach a facility-saturation rate equal to 50 percent of that in the United States, 1,352 self-storage facilities would need to be built in London within the next 10 years. This means building 2.6 facilities a week. If that's not a successful market waiting to happen, then I don't know what is."

This time next year Rodney, we'll be millionaires.

One day Warren didn't turn up for work. He didn't ring and he wasn't answering his phone at home. We thought about calling the police or going round to his house to see if he was okay.

Then a postcard arrived. The picture on the front was of a beach in Majorca. There was a Spanish postmark and other than the address and my name above it – written in Warren's scratchy handwriting – the postcard was blank. Warren thought he was Tim Robbins in *The Shawshank Redemption*. And I was Morgan Freeman. Maybe there was a tin hidden under a Spanish rock with a thousand dollars in it for me if my parole ever came through.

Two weeks later the owners of the company presumed Warren wasn't coming back and I was promoted to manager.

Ask your greengrocer or the man in the cornershop. Ask the milkman if you can find one. Go see Mister or Mrs Londis or the Goth girl with the sad face behind the counter at the Spa. They'll all tell you how quiet it's been. They'll pause between scanning your shopping to sigh and tell you how everyone takes the car out to the monster-market when they need a pint of milk or half a pound of apples these days. All those small shopkeepers, working a 72-hour week just to pay the rent and feed the kids. They wouldn't have been surprised when our small independent company was annexed by the self-storage superpowers.

We couldn't compete with the cheaper rates of hire, 24–hour access and CCTV cameras that the big corporate chains offered. They had Fancy Dan key codes and full insurance cover. Their staff dressed in colourful kids TV presenter dungarees and smiled like born again Christians.

While Warren drank sangria and sunburned his big jug ears on a Mediterranean beach, I watched as yet another derelict factory or church was knocked down and a new flat-packed building was unfolded and assembled in its place between all the tower blocks and superstores that dwarfed our pathetic bungalow of a warehouse, making the area look like it had been built out of cereal boxes by infant school children.

Every month it seemed like there was a new storage superstore setting up and stealing our customers, and in the words of Coldplay, they were all yellow.

Without going and taking a look now I couldn't tell you what colour the outside of our building is. My best guess would be Brick Red, or whatever colour concrete is. I can tell you with absolute confidence though, that there's a big sign nailed to the wall that says, or once said – in eighteen-inch high plastic silver letters – *2001: a storage space odyssey.*

For a while the name was clever. Amusing. Futuristic. Before it became topical. Then out of date, stupid and embarrassing. That was my era – the out of date, stupid and embarrassing years. I had to keep explaining the meaning behind the name and telling people it had nothing to do with David Bowie. Then the silver letters started to drop off, changing the company name and making nonsensical anagrams out of it. First 2001: a torage space odyssey, and then 2001: a   orage space odyssey. If only the date would fall off.

The space age didn't end with the sign. The interior of the building was painted silver and the doors to the storage units were numbered Apollo 1, Apollo 2, 3, 4 and so on. The computer in the Portakabin office was and still is referred to as HAL. Just like the supercomputer in the film that the company was named after. If you push the doorbell on the entry gates, *Also Sprach Zarathustra* by Richard Strauss – the opening music from that famous sc-fi movie – will play through a tinny speaker in the office. I often hear it in my sleep.

That's where I was when the man from the music mag rang. I was sitting on a chair that had lost its swivel and its backrest in a small Portakabin of an office just inside the front entrance of a badly-named storage facility that was dying on its arse. There was mould around the Portakabin's doorframe and a damp patch on the ceiling above my head that looked like a map of Burma or the birthmark on Mikhail Gorbachev's forehead. The office smelt of burnt lettuce and I thought I might be catching typhus and the kettle was broken. The flattened cardboard box that filled the broken Portakabin window space needed re-taping around the edges where it was coming away, letting in the elements and the spiders. On the flattened cardboard box it said FRAGILE. Sometimes I knew exactly how it felt. If it wasn't for Carl I might have opened a vein.

CARL

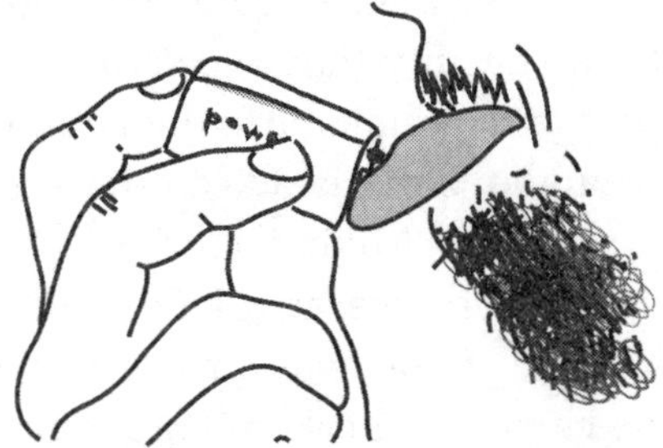

When I first met Carl he was licking a battery.

He was sitting in the corridor outside the unit he rented for his vast collection of junk. He was sorting a small box of nine-volt batteries into two piles: flat and not flat. Carl would tentatively touch the end of each battery with the tip of his tongue, playing battery Russian roulette. With every new mini electric shock he'd jerk his head back and then break into a smile, before adding the live battery to the right hand pile. A flat battery seemed to disappoint him.

Carl was videoing himself on a camcorder, set up on a rickety-looking tripod on the opposite side of the corridor. The camera captured Carl's reactions of joy or anticlimax on videotape so he could watch it all later.

Carl looked like a roadie in a movie about a rock band. He had a mullet haircut and a fat set of keys and tools and a Maglite torch hanging from the belt of a pair of faded jeans that showed more cleavage than a Page Three girl's blouse.

Some people might have said, no, not a roadie, what Carl looked like was a paedophile. If they saw Carl slow down outside a school to tie his shoelaces or to ask somebody the time, they might have called the police or taken Carl's photograph with their mobile phone. Just in case the Sunday tabloids ever needed it for a name and shame vigilante campaign.

Those suspicious idiots wouldn't have trusted Carl's beard. Carl's weird beard. It grew in patches in about three or four different shades of brown, grey and ginger. It looked false. You could be forgiven for tugging at Carl's beard to see if it was real.

Just like Disney with their forty-three year employee beard ban or New Labour when they instructed their hairy-faced MPs to shave, suspicious idiots looked at Carl and applied to him the principles that a Disney employee or a politician with a beard couldn't be trusted – they forgot that no politician could ever be trusted. They looked at Carl and they saw evil bearded baddies Charles Manson and Osama Bin Laden. They forgot about Jesus and Father Christmas. The sceptical fools saw Satan's evil goatee instead of God's comfy white curls.

Then there were Carl's thick-lensed glasses. And again, people jumped to conclusions. They chose to ignore Mahatma Gandhi's bottle specs and how they might have helped him see the possibilities of non-violence and equality. When some people first looked at Carl, rather than thinking of Ghandi healing the world's wrongs and making it a better place, they imagined instead a myopic pervert wanking himself blind in front of a sticky computer screen.

When I got to know him better, Carl would let me try on his thick-lensed glasses. They gave me an ice cream headache and left me with blurred vision for about two minutes. God knows what damage they were doing to Carl, hooked round his hairy ears all day long. Carl's hairy ears.

Carl pretty much always wore the same greasy red baseball hat, pulled down tight over the mullet that lurked beneath. His mullet that receded at the crown and front and advanced in long straw coloured locks down the back of his heavily creased and stained *My Cat Jeffers* sweatshirt, with its iron-on transfer picture of Carl's cat Jeffers on the front. Carl only had two shirts as far as I could tell. His My Cat Jeffers one and a yellow t-shirt that had a picture of Edinburgh Castle on the front. Carl was from Edinburgh. He was fifteen years younger than me and at the risk of sounding like a child, I'd go as far as to say that Carl is my best friend.

We bonded instantly, like superglue. When Carl couldn't afford to pay for the rental on his storage space, I gave him a job driving the company van. Carl's interview for the job consisted mainly of him showing me his BCG scar and the burn on his left shoulder in the shape of the gay holiday island Mykonos.

His training involved me showing him these three guitar chords:

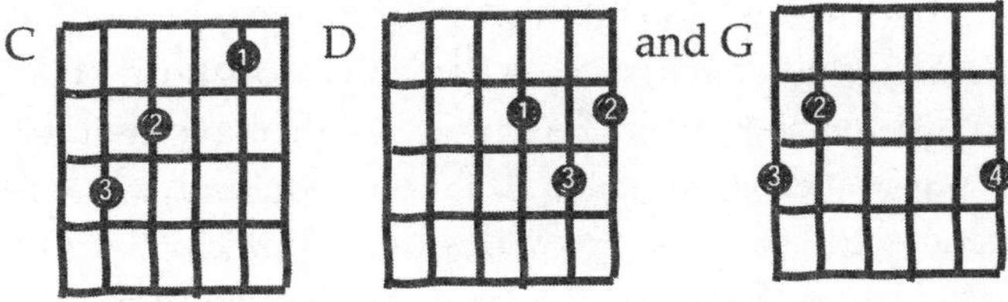

while he accompanied me by drumming on the desk and placing his hand in his armpit to make fart sounds.

On quiet days Carl and me would be noisy.

I acted more like a rock star with Carl than I ever did when I actually was one. I was always more Cliff than Keef Richard(s). All the time, while the rest of the band were snorting themselves into arrogance and self-importance or smashing up their hotel rooms. While they were emptying the mini bar into the toilet, blocking the bathroom sink with toilet paper and turning the taps on before morning check-out. While the drummer was dangling upside down from his hotel balcony, writing his name on the window of the room below with shaving foam and while the bass player and guitarist were gaffa taping the hotel furniture to the ceiling. All this time, I'd be sitting on my own watching CNN or washing my socks and pants in the hotel bathroom sink. The extent of my rock 'n' roll bad behaviour was to once unscrew a framed picture of a butterfly from a hotel wall and re-hang it upside down. Even then I felt guilty for weeks after and almost wrote a letter of apology.

But now on quiet days, Carl and me would be Mötley Crüe. We bought giant pump action water pistols and hid in empty storage units. Lying in wait to ambush and soak Janie when she came to look for us. We glued pound coins to the ground and waited for customers to try and pick them up, filming it all on Carl's camcorder.

Sometimes we'd open a bottle of champagne for no reason whatsoever. With nothing officially worth celebrating we'd shower each other with bubbly like we'd won the Grand Prix. We threw things at each other and played football in the corridor. If there was a box that was labelled *handle with care*, often we wouldn't. We were childish and we were stupid. If the Portakabin office hadn't been a bungalow, we would have thrown HAL out of the window.

On Fridays we'd go out after work and get as drunk as a hen night in Prague. One such night we got so drunk that we bought a mobile library.

Here's a picture of that vehicle:

When the government privatised the library service, the first things to go were the mobile libraries. You could find plenty for sale on the Internet auction sites. Or you could buy one from a man in a pub, like me and Carl did.

"An underpant-blue DAF Roadrunner van – no HGV required, tax and one year's MOT – windows in the roof, power assisted steering. An H-reg, with a hand basin, working bog, less than 45,000 miles on the Hickory Dickory, and books, hundreds of books: Dickens, Shakespeare, Potter and The Rings," the man in the pub said.

"We'll take it."

The fall of the public lending libraries had come when the public stopped borrowing from them, choosing instead to watch DVDs and play computer games. If the public really wanted to read books they could buy three in the shops and only have to pay for two of them. They could read the good bits online or edited and serialised in newspapers, or even via mobile phone text messages. Reading a whole book took too much time, too much commitment and concentration.

The books that *were* taken out of the library were usually returned overdue or unread and many more didn't come back at all. Never give people something for nothing, because they'll take it and they won't give it back. Out of every ten books borrowed from the library, only nine were ever returned. The bookshelves were emptying and the library service was collapsing. Which was when Whitehall stepped in.

"Start competing or prepare your books for privatisation or pulping." That's the gist of what those idiots in Whitehall said.

The libraries tried their best to survive. Opening on Wednesdays, not closing for lunch, selling coffees and cakes, holding amnesties on overdue books and *noisy days*. They offered cheap Internet access and free email addresses for members. The libraries cleared their bookshelf space to make room for more and more videos and DVDs and computer games.

But all their sleeping with the enemy was in vain and the public library became the private library. Those that weren't demolished were sold off to coffee and booze chains to be de-booked and reborn as library themed pubs and wine bars, places with names like The Paperback Writer and The Just Browse Inn. Novelty wine bars put up SILENCE PLEASE signs. Pubs employed whispering bespectacled bar staff.

We saw the introduction of the big out-of-town super libraries, where you could get a book out with your weekly shopping. People drove out to retail parks and to the 24–hour Tesco and Sainsbury's libraries. They took the tube into the West End to visit the Virgin MegaLibrary® and the ultra trendy Texas Book Depository on the Kings Road. Traditionalists and stuck-in-the-muds complained about the Americanisation of the British library system. To prove them right, people turned up in their thousands to watch and cheer *the biggest movie star in Hollywood* declare "the American Airlines British Library, now open!"

And, like I said, perhaps because they were on wheels, the mobile libraries were the first to go.

Me and Carl bought ours from a man in a pub – stop me if you think I'm repeating myself – we bought an underpant-blue Leyland DAF Roadrunner van, no HGV required, with tax and MOT, roof windows, power assisted steering, a hand basin and a chemical toilet.

On the back of the pant-blue van there was a bumper sticker that didn't say *Horn broken. Watch for finger* or *I love cats, they taste just like chicken*. Our bumper sticker was *your library is your paradise*.

The man in the pub said, "It's a quote from the Dutch

Humanist Desiderius Erasmus. He was known as the Prince of the Humanists. I read it in a book. From my library. Which is now your library. Cheers!"

Every weekend me and Carl would join the front line in the war between the small community book lenders and the big multinational and corporate ones. A real David and Goliath battle. Like something out of one of the stories on the shelves in the back of our van. Stories like *To Kill A Mockingbird* or *One Flew Over The Cuckoo's Nest,* or perhaps the heroic fairy tale of a small self-storage company taking on the might of a Big Yellow giant.

When me and Carl drove into town, AC/DC blasting out of our tinny old car stereo – like an ice cream van bringing 99s for the mind – people would rush out into the street to stop us and loan one.

Now, I don't want to carpet stereotype the entire neighbourhood as illiterate Neanderthals, but I think some of the members of our library hadn't read a lot of books before we drove into town. In our own little way, just like everybody said J K Rowling had done for schoolboys with her specky wizard books, Carl and me were getting people reading again. Putting something back was what we used to call it in the rock world.

Dickens, Shakespeare, Potter and The Rings were just the start of what our library had to offer. We lent people fat books, thin books, oversized and large print books. Brilliant books and terrible books, both versions of The Good Book, children's books and adult books. We lent them dictionaries and pictionaries, pop-up books and books you could take into the bath. We lent people self-help manuals and poetry anthologies, horror stories, sci-fi books, fantasy, romance, fiction and non, in hard back and paper. And nobody ever brought any of them back.

The clue to our impending downfall was in one of the few books still left on the shelf. In *Hamlet,* Shakespeare had written: *Neither a borrower, nor a lender be.* And he was at least half right. It seems our membership database turned out to be something of a flawed system. We hadn't asked people for two utility bills or a photocopy of their driver's licence or passport. We didn't even have anybody's name or address.

We thought about buying some more books to fill our emptying shelves. Perhaps stock some DVDs and computer games as well, or sell coffee and cakes. But then we'd just be making the same desperate mistakes as the old libraries had made.

So we gave up. We drove around, giving away whatever books were left. Choosing one book each to keep for ourselves, as a souvenir of our brief adventure in the library business. Carl chose *The Bloody History of Self-Surgery* and I went for something called *The Goth Cop.* We parked the empty pant-blue vehicle outside the most miserable sweetshop in the world and stuck one *for sale* sign in the windscreen and another on the back of a postcard in the window of the shop. With the money we'd get from the sale of the van, we said we were going to buy as much Scalextric as we could afford.

Going into the most miserable sweetshop in the world could be a soul-destroying experience. To see all the Mars Bars and Milky Ways on the shelves that had melted way back in the heat of a long-distant summer and then had hardened again, leaving the chocolate stuck to the wrappers, all misshapen and desiccated with a chalky sheen. As appetising as the dried-up white dog turds you don't see on the streets anymore. In the most miserable sweetshop in the world the Bountys had lost their taste of paradise and the Flakes really did taste like chocolate had never tasted before. Innocent children would skip into the shop without a care in the world, hand over their pocket money and leave two minutes later with their heads bowed, as depressed and cynical mini adults.

To the man behind the miserable sweetshop counter, the customer was not only always wrong but also an inconvenience and a menace. Every morning I'd go in for a pint of milk and a newspaper. I'd place my semi-skimmed on the counter next to my folded *Daily Mirror* and, although I knew I'd be wasting my time, I'd still smile at the man behind the counter. And I'd wait. And wait. Until, as usual I'd have to guess the price of my shopping, because the man behind the counter of the most miserable sweetshop in the world wasn't about to tell me. Or offer me a bag, say thank you, please or bye bye please come again, mind the step as you go. I'd leave the shop feeling more like apologising than thanking him for his service and I'd feel somehow guilty for having ruined his day by giving him money and taking things away from him.

After we placed our van for sale ad in the window, Carl asked me, "Don't you find it ironic that such a bitter man should choose to work in a sweetshop? Do you think he's always been so unhappy or do you suppose something happened that made him turn that way?"

I knew the man behind the counter hadn't always been a

misery guts. I could remember when things were sweeter in the sweetshop. I remembered what it was like in the most miserable sweetshop in the world before it got its name. I remembered how it used to be and I wanted those good old days back.

I'm not just talking about sugar and e number nostalgia. I'm not pining for the long lost tastes of Amazin' Raisin bars, blue minty Ice Breakers, traffic light lollipops and Salt 'N' Shake crisps. Those good old days when Snickers were still Marathons, Lion Bars were Picnics and M & Ms were Treets. I'm not just hankering after a naïve confectionery past full of Toot Sweets and candy canes. When the Milky Bar Kid could fire his cap gun at a boy in a Red Indian outfit without a stiff letter from the Advertising Standards Authority or the Commission For Racial Equality. Those bygone days when you could pop a Love Heart in your mouth and it didn't say TXT ME or B MY MSN. It was more than that.

Something had made the Curly Wurlys lose their curl and the Crunchies lose their crunch. Something had burst the Aeros' bubbles, ruined the Black Magic's magic and the Quality Street's quality. In the most miserable sweetshop in the world the crisps were soft and the ice cream fridge was empty with a shoal of silverfish doing sticky freestyle lengths in the orange, lemon and strawberry of a melted Rocket ice-lolly at the bottom of it. Nobody was ever going to win the lottery with a ticket bought from this shop. No one would match three £5,000s on a scratch card from this counter. There'd be no please or thank you, no good morning, no cheerio, no dogs allowed, no more than two children at a time.

And it was all my fault.

THE MOST MISERABLE SWEETSHOP IN THE WORLD

This is Anne.

Anne is the wife of the man behind the counter of the most miserable sweetshop in the world. Like me Anne had once rented space for a dead parent's belongings.

As I said before, you can tell a lot about people from what they put into storage. I could pitch up a tent at the end of a pier and read your junk for you, like tealeaves or runes. Spread out your excess keepsakes on a trestle table and I'll tell you all about yourself. Go on. Call it therapy. Lay back on that couch you've just put away and let me work my magic.

When Anne brought in her mother's collection of jigsaw puzzles of the Royal Family and cassettes of Margaret Thatcher speeches, already I was getting a clear picture of the dead woman. The frumpy knitting patterns, latch hook rugs and the cardboard boxes full of assorted dowdy clothes and sensible shoes told me the rest. Anne put all her dead mother's stuff into storage. Including her dead mother.

I don't imagine it was her dying wish for her final resting place to be in a cheap plastic urn on the top of a pile of yellowing back issues of the Daily Mail in a crappy storage warehouse. I guessed Anne hadn't liked her mother all that much.

The last thing Anne threw on the pile was a picture, painted and signed by Anne. It was a portrait of a severe looking old trout, clearly not enjoying the experience of having her picture painted. The woman in the picture was probably in her late seventies or early eighties but in spite of her age and the fine detail of Anne's brushwork, there were no laugh lines on the woman's face. Not one. The old bag had clearly never smiled.

It was a good painting. The eyes followed me around what little room there was in Anne's rented space. And I'd never felt so hated. Nothing personal. Anne's mother hated all men. Every man her daughter had brought home would have been stared at in the same way. Anne's mother would have questioned and cross-examined them all under a hypothetical hundred-watt light bulb for suitability. Fingerprinted, mug-shotted and strip-searched them and had the backs of their mouths swabbed for DNA. None of them would have been good enough for her daughter and none of them came back for more.

Anne put some of her own stuff into storage too. Her collection of holiday brochures and wedding shop catalogues, a pile of sketchbooks and some bizarrely coloured paintings and a dozen or so videos of films that seemed to be almost entirely about escape: whether it be from prison, the Germans or the Planet of the Apes.

When Anne's mother had become ill, Anne had put her search for Mister Right on hold to look after her. The two women played Scrabble in the afternoons and filled in a whole pile of crossword puzzle books. They made latch hook rugs together and played aptly named card games like Old Maid and Solitaire.

And then, on the eve of the new millennium and an impending catastrophic computer apocalypse, with just one minute to go before Big Ben's bongs, Anne's mother kicked the bucket.

What a way to go.

A thousand fireworks lit up the New Year's sky as Anne's mother went to meet her maker. Anne cracked open a bottle of Moët and Chandon to celebrate. Double bubble.

After the funeral Anne boxed up her mother's belongings: the clothes, the Scrabble, the Thatcher cassettes and the empty champagne bottle. She put everything into storage along with what was left of her cremated mother and she took a long deserved holiday.

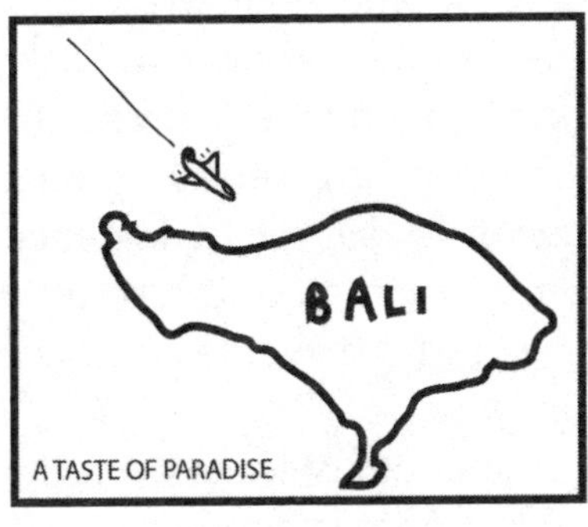

WHERE THE SWEETS HAVE NO NAME

It was a brand new century. The computers didn't crash. It was safe to fly again. *Painting Beautiful Bali,* the holiday brochure said. *Fourteen glorious days in paradise – for beginners and experienced painters alike, from doodler to Dali.*

Anne packed her bags and flew to Bali. She'd wake up early in the mornings to paint the vivid blue sun rising from behind all the fantastic pink temples, yellow volcanoes and purple mountains. And then when the sun set behind the horizon she painted it all over again, in the many inappropriate colours of her crazy mind's rainbow.

Anne decided to leave her camera in her suitcase and draw or paint everything she saw instead. All the landscapes, lush tropical forests and rice terraces, the dolphins and whale sharks and some of the three hundred species of birds: Sea eagles, sandpipers, white herons and blue kingfishers, cuckoos, wood swallows, sparrows and starlings. And all the friendly Balinese people the brochure told her she'd meet. Anne soaked it all up like a Battenberg.

At her holiday art classes she'd learn traditional Balinese painting techniques and all about local colours. Then Anne would mix and match them with her own bonkers palette. Anne's dramatic orange and yellow striped bull that looked like a tiger, lost in a vast field of terracotta and tangerine rice in front of a forest of salmon pink palm trees, where the patchwork herons nest in all their aubergine glory. That particular insane masterpiece currently sits in a darkened storage room next to another picture of a black volcanic sandy beach, painted in a strawberry jam red that you can almost taste.

When Anne and her Bali art class ran out of things to paint, they got on a coach and drove off in search of new things. They went to a cliff-top temple to witness the spectacular Monkey Dance. A dance telling the story of Sita, the wife of Rama. The dance told of how Sita is kidnapped by Rama's archenemy Alengka and taken to his palace. Rama enlists the help of the red monkey king Sugriwa to help him find his kidnapped wife and the pair of them seek out the magical powers of the white monkey Hanoman. Rama gives Hanoman his ring to prove his identity to Sita when he finds her. When Hanoman eventually finds Sita, he gives her the ring and tries to destroy the palace where Sita is a prisoner but is captured and placed in a ring of straw and set alight. This was the most spectacular part of the cliff-top show, as the white monkey danced in and around the burning straw, kicking the flames away and chasing the bad guys out of town so that Sita and Rama could be reunited.

Anne's favourite part of the Kecak Dance though, was the one hundred moustachioed and bare-chested Balinese men in tied head cloths and checked shorts. They sat in circles chanting and singing noisily, their arms thrust towards the heavens and their fingers outstretched like acid housers off their tits in a field in the second summer of love. They were the show's orchestra and choir and they also represented wind and fire and such like. They gave Anne the horn.

The following morning, the art class was asked to paint what they'd seen. Anne painted a sherbet lemon dib dab King Kong with a friendly bearded face a bit like Richard Branson or Rolf Harris.

This is Guntur.

Guntur was Anne's art teacher.

When Anne met Guntur it was like opening the first Cadbury's crème egg of the year.

Guntur had a great moustache. Not a Hitler or a Stalin or any of those other hairy lipped evil bastards. Guntur had nothing nasty to hide behind his tash except the face of a gentle baby Jesus and a smile that was infectious like a yawn. As his smile broke from under Guntur's moustache it revealed his filed down dogteeth. That was something they did in Bali; Anne had read about it on the plane. Filing down the teeth of the pubescent child. It had made her wince at twenty thousand feet. Guntur's upper canine teeth had been filed down in an elaborate ceremony as soon as his voice had begun to break. To symbolically shoo away his animal nature and to rid him of the six weaknesses of the flesh: lust, greed, anger, drunkenness, confusion and jealousy. Guntur's six weaknesses were gone now and all that was left were his strengths: his kindness, his enthusiasm, his patience and understanding. All that and a body cut like Mr. Gay Universe.

What was Balinese for Phwoooorrrr? Anne wondered.

Guntur had a whole holiday sketchpad all to himself. Anne had drawn over fifty different pictures of him. With his magnificent moustache and infectious smile. She'd sketched and painted him laughing and singing and fast asleep on the beach with his bronzed skin soaking up the rays and giving Anne the horn.

"Bold strokes, Anne," Guntur said as he stood behind her with both arms around her waist guiding her brush. "That is beautiful, Anne, the colour of your sky is unusual but still most beautiful."

"Thank you," she said. And *phwoooorrrr*, she wanted to say.

If only it was in her phrase book.

If only Anne knew what to say to her teacher in his own language.

Something sexy.

Something dirty.

Anne could have just said something seductive in English of course – I'm sure it's possible – and Guntur spoke and understood English well, but the tourist guidebooks always tell you that the local people love it when you try to speak their language. With Guntur in the hotel room next to Anne's, she could have whispered it to him from her bed and then put a glass between her ear and the wall and awaited his response.

Dirty words continued to fail Anne. Her holiday was almost over. The 747 would be touching down in London to be emptied of its passengers, cleaned and refueled for its return flight to Bali, where it would again be emptied of passengers, cleaned and refueled. That would happen another seven or eight times and then the airplane would be ready for Anne. She'd have to pack her bags and get on the airport shuttle bus and then it would all be over for her and Guntur. All those afternoons and evenings spent with her mother playing Scrabble and filling in crosswords had done nothing for Anne's conversational skills; she was excellent at word games but knew nothing about words.

She knew the Balinese for *thank you* and *good day*. She could ask *what's the price?* She knew that *kantor pos* was the post office. She could point at Guntur and say *Guntur enak,* which translated roughly as *delicious*. But he'd think she was a halfwit. From her trips to the local market Anne had learned the phrase *saya tidak mau,* which meant *I don't want* and that was fine for turning away the Tommy Hilfibber perfume and Roleks wristwatch sellers in the street outside her hotel, but it was rubbish for what she needed to say to Guntur. *I don't want* was useless to Anne, because Anne *did* want, oh boy, she really did, more than anything in years.

If Anne had taken a look in the drawer of her hotel bedside table she might have found inspiration, divine inspiration courtesy of the Gideons, who'd been clocking up their Air Miles, perhaps on a stopover to Sydney or Perth. If Anne had looked in her hotel drawer she might have found some helpful advice.

In all these different places:

Leviticus 19:18, Matthew 5:43, Mark 12:31. And also, Luke 10:27, Romans 13:9, Galatians 5:14 and James 2:8.

Pop next door now and ask him if you can borrow a cup of sugar or his hedge trimmers, Anne.

"Come in," he'll say, and he'll ask you if you'd like a drink and you can say yes and then you can plead with him to take you, take you, right here right now, on the bathroom floor and in front of the mini bar, out onto the balcony in the fading light of the setting Bali sun and back inside again, onto the freshly made hotel bed. Tell him you love him you love him, screaming in his ears so high-pitched that he can't hear it, but a hundred Bali street dogs – Dalmatian, Dingo, Spitz, Chow-Chow, Samoyed, Boarder Collie and Basenji, all crossbred into one Balinese super canine – can and will hear your screams from the other side of the island. And maybe they'll come running to your rescue out of a doggie misinterpretation of all the screaming and your love cries of *"NO, NO, STOP, NO!"* And they'll come leaping through the open hotel window to save you and they'll find a man built like Mr. Gay Universe all over you like the rash his moustache will leave you with in the morning. And he'll be kissing your heaving alabaster breasts, licking the salty beads of sweat that glisten and reflect against the shine of his filed down upper canines and his skin that smells and shines like a new candle. Do it Anne, it's in the Bible, love thy neighbour. Just as he loves you: passionately, far-fetched and filthy, like a passage from an Alan Titchmarsh novel.

Look in the drawer Anne!

BALI SUGAR

On Anne's final day in paradise Anne and Guntur were in the gardens outside the hotel.

"Can you smell the flowers, Anne?" Guntur asked. "Hibiscus and Jasmine, Magnolias and this one is called Bougainvillea." He picked the flower with its pinky purple and crimson leaves, described by many as the most versatile and varied in colour of all plants, and put it in the hair of the artist who could be described in a similar fashion. And then he kissed her. The next morning Anne cancelled her flight home to England.

AFTER THE SUGAR RUSH

Anne had framed the front page of her local free newspaper that told the story of how her holiday romance had blossomed like that Bougainvillea and led to a spectacular Balinese wedding. The paper told how the happy couple had then come back to England and opened a newsagents just off the High Street. A newsagents that soon made the front page again when it was voted as *Local Small Business of the Year*.

The shop had become famous for its friendly service from the sweet kindhearted man from Bali. People would pass by other confectioners and tobacconists so that they could purchase their cigarettes and chocolate from Guntur. If they were going to get tooth decay and lung cancer, they'd prefer it to come from someone polite. Possibly the only polite shopkeeper left in London.

The newspaper got a bit carried away with itself in its Local Small Business of the Year piece and suggested that Guntur should have his statue carved and placed on the fourth plinth in Trafalgar Square or his portrait hung in the National Gallery. Damien Hurst should cut Guntur into sections, the paper joked, and preserve him in glass cases full of formaldehyde.

A KINDA SURPRISE

Inspired by the paper's witty suggestions, Anne decided to paint a picture of her husband. She'd put it in a nice frame and give it to him as a surprise present on his next birthday. Anne's storage space would be her artist's studio.

She began by experimenting with many different art techniques and materials. She used linseed oil based paints, watercolours and acrylics. She tried milk and egg based paints, gouache and pastel, poster paint and spray paint, ink and charcoal. Anne used paint rollers and pencils and pens, felt-tips and quills made from scabby pigeon feathers. She painted with her fingers and thumbs and took her shoes and socks off to paint Guntur with her toes like Daniel Day Lewis in that film.

Anne tried painting Guntur's face on driftwood and cardboard and on an old door she found in a skip. One afternoon I watched her step out into the corridor outside her storage unit and throw paint back into the room and onto the canvas like she was Jackson Pollock. She tried caricature: extending Guntur's nose, giving him Prince Charles ears and making his moustache look like the head of a broom.

She painted pictures of Guntur by the sea, in fields of barley, on a horse, on a boat, on the moon. She painted him in sunshine and in the rain, completely nude and dressed in long white robes surrounded by doves. And she wasn't happy with any of them. Anne felt that each new picture was as rubbish as that old skip door. She just couldn't capture the man's good nature and his extraordinary humanity, what she called *that Gunturness*.

While Anne was working on her husband's surprise birthday present, Guntur was left to run the shop alone. He never complained. Anne would come home with paint in her hair and Guntur never asked why. He would already have run a bath for her, with bubbles and candles and the smell of lavender and chamomile in the steam. After her bath Anne would come downstairs to find Guntur laying the table for the evening meal and next to Anne's plate he would have placed a single Bougainvillea in a tall glass of water on the kitchen table. The same pinky purple and crimson colour as the one he'd picked for Anne on the night of their first Bali kiss. Guntur had planted, potted, composted and re-potted, watered and sprayed it with fairy liquid to chase away greenfly. Talking to the plant every morning in Indonesian, Balinese and English in a tiny makeshift greenhouse at the back of the sweetshop. Just so he could pick it again and put it in a tall glass for the woman he loved. For pudding Guntur would have brought home some ice cream from the shop and he would have arranged Love Heart sweets on the top of the ice cream to read, DREAM GIRL or FOR EVER.

Anne was close to giving up on her husband's portrait when somebody put a card in the sweetshop window for a primary school art department that was selling off its old stock of art supplies. Anne thought she might at last capture Guntur's childlike wonder if she used children's paint and so she bought two-dozen grey plastic containers of powder paint and fat wooden brushes. She stacked them up in her storage unit ready to begin work on one final Guntur portrait.

It was while Anne painted this latest picture that Guntur began to morph into a grouch. He started to communicate with his customers only in Neanderthal grunts and half-hearted head gestures. He didn't bother to restock the shelves any more and dust settled and cobwebs formed. He stopped lifting the metal riot proof shutters when he opened the shop in the morning, leaving them rolled down over the window all day. He didn't flip the small sign over in the door, so it permanently said CLOSED and the tinkle of the little doorbell that had previously welcomed customers into the shop was now more of a death toll.

When Anne was finally happy with her powder painting she showed it to me. She said that she was particularly pleased with Guntur's moustache, which she'd painted by mixing equal parts Red Umber, Burnt Sienna and Ash Grey.

"Which is funny," Anne said. "Because I don't remember buying any Ash Grey." And then she went home to her husband, who she told me hadn't been himself lately. She said that she hoped she wasn't about to lose another man. A love loss that for once she wouldn't be able to blame on her misandrist mother.

Now. It's often been said that Balinese people are among the friendliest, most gracious and hospitable people in the world and Guntur was a fine example of that. So what was it that happened to Guntur that made him change into someone so grumpy and ill tempered? Was it the British weather? The people? The old biddies and the busybodies who he'd heard saying it was disgusting how he was married to a woman twice his age and referring to him as a mail order husband who was only after a British passport and Anne's money. Is that what turned Guntur? Or was it the relentless shoplifters? The drunks who pissed in his doorway every Friday and Saturday night? Maybe it was the illiterate and geographically challenged racists who banged on his shop window every time they passed and who painted PACKYS OUT on his door.

Perhaps as Anne's painting of Guntur had become closer to his true likeness, the happier Anne had painted him, the more miserable he'd become. The Dorian Gray effect. The closer Anne got to painting Guntur's happiness the more miserable he became. Newton's Third Law – for every action there is an opposite reaction. Anne paints a happy face, Guntur gets an unhappy one. That would be a clever idea.

Or.

Just before Anne started painting that final Guntur picture I was hiding behind her pyramid of powder paint containers. It was on one of Carl and my quiet days and I was about to call Carl on his mobile and ask him to come and look for me. I was going to ambush him with a tea tray loaded with water bombs. As I got into position I slipped on one of Anne's mother's Thatcher cassettes and knocked the paint pyramid over, crashing to the floor, spilling the powder everywhere.

I quickly got a dustpan and brush and cleared up the mess, scooping the paints back into their relevant containers as best as I could, mixing some of the colours and creating brand new ones as I did so. I mixed the Royal Blue with the Pretty Pink, the Racing Green with the Red Umber and the Burnt Sienna with Anne's dead mother. I don't imagine it was her dying wish, to have her remains scattered in a crappy storage warehouse but as the old witch's eyes followed me around the room while I swept up her ashes, ashes that Anne would use to paint Guntur's moustache, Anne's mother's miserable portrait face, a face without laugh lines, seemed to smile.

Why not store your clothes on a seasonal basis. Pack away your winter coats, scarves and gloves for the summer months and your Bermuda shorts and Hawaiian shirts for the winter.

JANIE

Since my wife left me, there were only two women I'd spent any real time alone with. One was my doctor, who'd cupped my testicles in the palm of her hand and had her finger up my arse – but still no date. The other was Janie Maplin.

Janie was our office Girl Friday, Monday, Wednesday and every other Saturday. She came in to type out invoices, order stationery and tidy up the mess I'd made of things on Tuesday, Thursday and every other other Saturday. Janie was like the punch line to that old Chinese proverb joke we used to tell at school: *Woman who go to bed at night with coat hanger in mouth wake up with smile on face.* On first meeting Janie, you might presume she was either very happy about something, American, on drugs, or perhaps a bit simple.

Janie Maplin had been Janie Tandy until she married Nick Maplin. Janie Tandy and Nick Maplin. It should have been a match made in electronic hobby shop Heaven. It wasn't.

We were in the pub. Just the three of us: Janie, Carl and me. Carl was at the bar and Janie was talking about her husband.

She told me about her wedding day. How she'd swapped cheap rings with Nick Maplin in a church that she said smelled like a hotel drawer. The wedding took place on Janie's 24th birthday and she regretted it before she'd reached her 25th.

Every night Janie would cook her husband's meals and watch them turn cold while he was out getting drunk and eating kebabs. She chose, bought, washed and ironed his clothes for him to puke his kebab down the front of and she stayed in on Saturday nights to record unimportant Third Division boring and goal-less football matches that he had no intention of ever watching, over videos of her favourite films of all time.

"By the time I'd booked the caterers, chosen the flowers and paid for the cake, it was too late," she said. "You know those TV programmes with the CCTV footage of the Saturday night piss-heads attacking people for no reason in the High Street? That's him. That's my husband. He once pushed a pint glass into a student's face because he thought he'd jumped the queue for the pool table. I saw him do it. It terrified me. So much blood and he couldn't stop laughing. Like it was the funniest thing he'd ever seen."

"What does he do?" I asked her.

"He's a wanker."

"No, I mean for a job."

"He's a professional wanker."

"Apart from all that though, does he have some kind of day job?"

"You know all the graffiti round here?" Janie said.

"God yes. If you stand still for too long, you'll be tagged yourself. I saw a sausage dog the other day, tied up outside a post office, graffiti'd from sausage nose to sausage tail in white spray paint," I was doing my graffiti comedy shtick for her. "Is that your husband?" I said. "Which one is he? Is he MIDAZ or STREEK? He's not FAZD is he?"

The graffiti we were talking about here wasn't elaborate Arts Council or education authority commissioned community art. This graffiti wasn't a colourful mural brightening up a skate park, or a breathtaking fresco depicting the rich tapestry of an eclectic and funky neighbourhood. Neither was it the quaint *Kilroy was here* or Mr. Chad with his googly eyes and banana nose hanging over a Second World War wall, saying, *Wot no Spam?* This wasn't *we luv The Beatles, they're fab and gear,* daubed in Tippex by Italian tourists on an Abbey Road Studios zebra crossing. The graffiti we were talking about was just badly painted, illegible scribble.

"Nick's the one who cleans the graffiti off the walls and fences," Janie said. "He removes the tags from the white vans and the garage doors, from the road signs and the sausage dogs. And also from the harder and more dangerous to get at places, like the rooftops and railway bridges, heaven pieces they call those ones, or giraffiti.

"The trouble was, his one-man graffiti clean-up campaign was so successful that he had nothing left to paint over. He was driving himself out of business. Which was when he had the idea of hiring groups of teenagers to re-tag the walls he'd whitewashed over days before. So that he could charge people to paint over them again. And on and on it goes. After paper rounds and mobile phone theft, Nick is probably the largest provider of local youth employment." Janie told me. "But please, don't ever tell anybody about any of this. Or any of the other things I've said. People would only think I was a softheaded fool for staying with a man I couldn't stand. Making lemonade out of lemons, or whatever it is."

Carl came back from the bar with a round of drinks.

"I better go after this one," Janie said. "He'll be expecting dinner."

When Nick dropped Janie off at work the following Monday in his little van with the ladder on the top and the paint in the back – I'd always thought he was a painter and decorator or a builder or something – Janie had her arm in a sling. She said she'd slipped over on a drain cover in the rain. It hadn't rained for ages.

TWO GRAND PRIX

Carl's Formula One Williams BMW was under-steering badly out of the hairpin bend at Silverstone and he lost control. He came off the track at 150 miles per hour, his car skidding and somersaulting as it ploughed a furrow through a line of spectators. I cruised nonchalantly past in my American fag packet red Schumacher Ferrari, my fist raised triumphantly as I took the chequered flag to the cheers of the capacity grandstand crowd of jubilant fans playing on a small ghetto blaster in the corner of the room.

We'd sold our pant-blue van and kept our promise to blow the money on plastic racing cars. And our Scalextric set-up was pretty spectacular. We had a four lane wide track, laid out like a Grand Prix circuit in one of the empty storage spaces. Sometimes it was Silverstone other times it was laid out like the Nurburgring, or Carl's favourite, Japan's Suzuka track, with its twenty corners, spoon and hairpin curves and I don't know how many tiny plastic Japanese race fans. Carl liked to get the detail right. From the grandstands and the flags, to the advertising hoardings selling tobacco everywhere but Silverstone. And then there were the plastic trees he planted around the track, the pit lanes and the little plastic pit crews. At the side of Carl's Suzuka track there was even a miniature fun fair.

We could have played Scalextric all day long. The smell of the hot track's plastic was intoxicating. It was so much more exciting than the real Grand Prix. More overtaking, more crashes, more skidding and somersaulting, ploughing furrows through lines of spectators. And when did you ever get to see either of the Schumacher brothers or Fernando Alonso get down on their bended knees, put their tongue onto the track and squeeze on the throttle till they felt the electricity surging through their tongues, like Carl would often do?

One day, during a particularly crash-filled race, an out of breath Carl said,

"Jesus Christ, I'm exhausted just walking back and forth picking the cars up. I'm so unfit, and look at that." Carl lifted his t-shirt and patted his belly. "I look pregnant."

I lifted my shirt and joined Carl in the belly patting. I wasn't so slim myself. On a scale of One to Elvis, these were my Vegas years. Stuck in the same damn building day after day after day, snacking myself to eventual toilet death, while Colonel Tom Parker frittered away my fortune in the slot machines in the lobby downstairs.

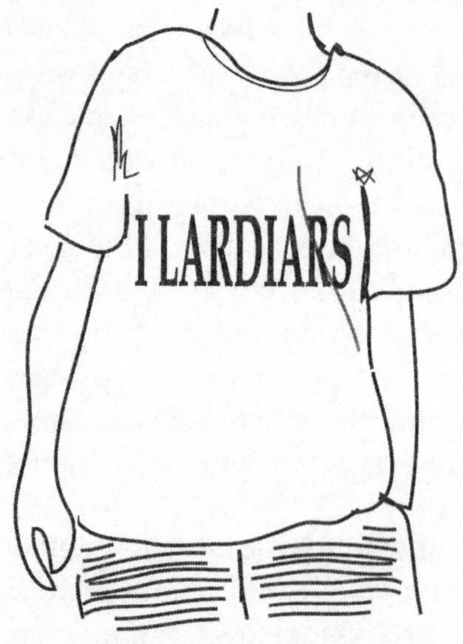

This is the reason that reforming old rock and pop bands is such a bad idea and also at the same time so lucrative for people like Colonel Tom. People love a freak show. They'll buy a ticket just to check out the singer's receding hairline and

see how fat the bass player's become. It makes the audience feel better about their own mortality. About their own expanding and receding waist and hairlines. To see what all those years off the cocaine and blowjobs and on the cheesy chips and Hobnobs have done to their once skinny musical heroes. That's why Johnny Cash always dressed in black. Not as he said, for all the oppressed people of the world, but because Johnny knew that black was a slimming colour.

"Maybe it's time to sort ourselves out." I said to Carl.

He patted his belly once more, as if bidding farewell to an old friend for the final time and said,

"What are you suggesting? Push-ups? A game of squash? Football?"

"I haven't played football since school. I won a medal, it's the only thing I've ever won," I said. "I was the school team super-sub. In a football tournament that I have no recollection of ever actually kicking a ball in. Technically, I got a medal for sitting on a bench and watching."

I enjoyed sport at school but I wasn't particularly any good at it. I once swam a total of a mile in ten-yard widths, on the day that I discovered I could sleep while swimming, a feat I haven't managed to repeat since. Even so, I was never entered into any actual swimming races. Maybe because I didn't know how to dive and also had trouble staying in lane once I'd belly flopped into the water.

When I was a kid I was a real rake. Gardeners would step on my feet and I'd spring up and knock their teeth out with my head. I used to tiptoe from changing room to pool, my arms folded tight across my pigeon chest, my pea-sized biceps tensed to appear slightly bigger until I was under cover of water – just in case any girls might be looking, looking and laughing. I really was the puny weakling who the musclemen liked to have around to put all their hard work in the gym into perspective. Charles Atlas, the ninety-seven pound weakling who became *the worlds most perfectly developed man* would have sympathised with me I'm sure.

World famous bodybuilder Charles Atlas, or Angelo Charles Siciliano as he was at the time, was, like myself, a milk-pale and stick-thin kid who, after having the sand of Coney Island Beach kicked into his face once too often, had come up with a system for rebuilding his body in the privacy of his own home, without the need for expensive gym equipment. He called it Dynamic Tension, an exercise regime that involved tensing your muscles and using the resistance created to, I don't actually know what, I'm not a PE teacher. But when I was about thirteen, I tried Charles' Dynamic Tension bodybuilding system to beef myself up. I used to tense my arms, pumping some imaginary iron, pulling on invisible ropes. Rowing a boat that wasn't there. With my skinny body clenched like a fist and my face all taught and red with effort, if anyone had walked in on me, it might have appeared as though I were attempting to deliberately shit my pants.

Needless to say, I soon lost interest. Sports without sports equipment can be pretty dull. And I stayed skinny and never got to have my perfectly proportioned physique used to model for over seventy-five statues, including one of George Washington in New York City, like my hero Charles Atlas had done.

Next I got quite heavily into long distance running. I wasn't very good at that either but I was very keen and it was the middle of the 1970s, a time when winning wasn't as important as taking part and failing miserably, so my efforts were applauded and encouraged. My running heroes were 3,000 metres World record holder Brendan Foster, Alf Tupper (the *Tough of The Track* from the *Victor* comic) and Smith, the title character in the Alan Sillitoe story *The Loneliness of The Long Distance Runner*. I think the fact that all my heroes were tough northern whippet owners and I was a southern shandy-drinking poodle-fancier was what stopped me truly fulfilling my Olympic dream.

"Come and have a look at something." I said to Carl, who was still looking at his potbelly.

I showed Carl the gym equipment somebody had stored away next door to our indoor Scalextric racetrack. There was a treadmill, a rowing machine, two exercise bikes, a mini trampoline and various balls, skipping ropes and weights.

"All this get fit equipment going to waste," I said. "The man who brought it in took away a chocolate fountain, a popcorn maker and one of those lean mean grilling machines."

"His get fat equipment." Carl said.

"It seems a shame to waste it." I said.

THE WARM UP

I'm not sure if you can weigh wind but I reckon between us we lost a good stone and a half in those flatulent first five minutes warming our bodies up. We began with a few simple star-jumps and windmills and then we got stuck into the cycling, rowing, skipping and weight lifting.

"Should… this… be…nnngggghh…uuhhh… hurting this much?" Carl said.

"Remember Jane Fonda and her burn?" I said.

"Nnnhhgghh…more like Henry Fonda, I can hardly… eeuuughh… breathe." Carl stuck out his bottom lip as he tried to blow away the sweat droplet hanging from the end of his nose.

"It must be working." I said.

"I think I'm going to die," Carl said. "I don't want to go like this."

"Shut up and row."

We pulled on those stupid oars, me in my ill-fitting tracksuit, our bones snapping and popping and crackling like a bonfire. We were stretching and retching, pumping and trumping ourselves to death on the off chance we might be able to somehow shape ourselves into Peter Andre.

Approximately one exhausting hour of medieval muscle torture later, me and Carl went to the pub. On our return we found a small boy carrying this sign:

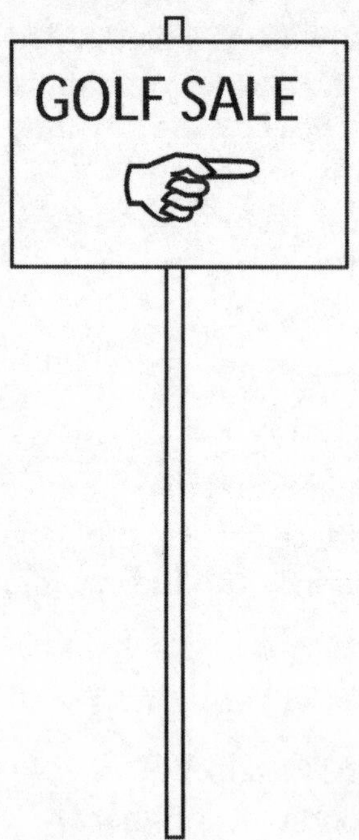

I don't know, you try and improve yourself with a bit of simple exercise and somebody sets up a golf sale. The finger pointed towards a storage unit where a small queue had formed to buy clubs, balls, tees, golf bags, sports casual clothing and other golfing paraphernalia from a man named Jeff. What the eff was Jeff playing at? At first I was furious; we didn't have a licence for an impromptu indoor sports market. But luckily for Jeff I was too tired from all my exercising to kick his face in and I let him finish serving his remaining customers. On condition that Jeff's son, who was holding the sign, buggered off and that Jeff gave me a good deal on a set of clubs and a couple of pairs of plaid pants. Forget the multi gym, Carl and me were going to play golf.

We didn't need a roomful of machinery to get fit. Eighteen holes and all the walking between would be all the exercise we'd need. All the rockers were doing it. Alice Cooper, Iggy Pop, Metallica, The Offspring, Tommy Lee, Puff Daddy, Bob Dylan, Meatloaf, Lou Reed. Golf was the new heroin.

And the trousers – to quote Tiger Woods – "they're *greeeeaaaaaaat!*"

We took our new golf clobber into the office and I logged onto the web to check out the rules of the game, this first bit is what I expected to find:

GOLF: INTRODUCTION TO THE GAME

A game in which a ball is struck with a club from an area known as the teeing ground to a second area with a hole in it and a flag, known as the 'putting green'. The object of the game is to hit the ball from the teeing ground into the hole in the fewest number of strokes. A round of golf consists of playing 18 of these holes.

Simple.

And then I read on:

ETIQUETTE

1. Don't move, talk or stand close to a player making a stroke.

2. Don't play until the group in front is out of the way.
3. Always play without delay. Leave the putting green as soon as all players in your group have holed out.
4. Invite faster groups to play through.
5. Replace divots. Smooth any footprints left in bunkers.
6. Don't step on the line of another player's putt.
7. Don't drop clubs on the putting green.
8. Replace the flagstick carefully.

Fuck off… *Alice? Iggy? Tommy Lee?* Etiquette? I don't think so. I think they're going to be leaving divots where they want to leave them, stepping all over other players' putts, dropping clubs, using the flags as javelins, snorting Charlie off the green, driving the golf cart into the lake.

The etiquette rules went on for about another fifty pages. Stuff about lost balls, casual water, loose impediments, balls at rest, deflected and unplayable balls, ball interfering and teeing off. I expect if you tried reading any of those rules to Puff Daddy or Meat Loaf *they'd* be pretty tee'd off. You'd be the one resting your balls after they'd been interfered with, deflected and rendered lost or unplayable.

Have you ever tried cutting a golf ball in half? I have. Me and Carl did it a few times one empty afternoon at work. Almost every time we cut into the ball the resulting explosion of rubber nearly took my eye out. For anyone that isn't au fait with golf ball surgery: the modern ball consists of a solid rubber core wrapped in high-tension rubber thread and covered in dimpled Gutta Percha from the Isonandra tree. When you cut one in half, the high-tension rubber thread will eventually panic and start uncoiling at high speed, shooting off in different directions, stinging your fingers and possibly blinding you.

You have been warned.

GOLF BALL SCIENTIFIC EXPERIMENT NUMBER 2:
THE MAGIC RISING GOLF BALL

You'll need:

1 Golf ball

1 empty glass jar and lid

Uncooked rice

How it's done

Place the golf ball at the bottom of the jar. Fill the jar with the uncooked rice to about an inch or so from the top of the jar. Close the lid. Shake the jar back and forth (not up and down).

Watch the magic

As the golf ball rises to the surface.

How does it happen?

No two pieces of matter can occupy the same space at the same time and as you shake the jar the grains of rice move closer together, they settle in the jar and push the ball upward. Now let's play golf.

Both Carl and I had the same golf handicap of not being able to play golf. It was a very long first game. More experienced players stuck behind us, grew more and more impatient as a golfing gridlock built up around the course.

At the 13th hole it began to rain, which was when I discovered that not only was I the luckiest man in the world but I was playing golf with the unluckiest. First I hit a hole in one – about a 60,000 to one chance of that happening – and then Carl was struck by lightning in the bunker and again on the fairway of the 14th.

As he lay flat on his back on the soggy grass smelling like a singed eyebrow, Carl said that he'd actually quite enjoyed the lightning strikes. He said it was like licking a thousand batteries all at once or putting his tongue on an actual Silverstone size Scalextric track.

That was the end of our keep fit regime. Carl had an afternoon in hospital with temporary amnesia, superficial burns and hair like Albert Einstein and we took it all as a sign that exercise was for other people. We decided we'd get fit slowly instead of quick and our exercise routine would consist almost entirely of using the push-me-pull-you shop doors instead of the automatic ones, and walking on the down escalators instead of standing still. I for one expected to see Peter Andre looking back at me from the mirror before much longer.

One day Janie came into work wearing an eyepatch.

She said she'd picked up an inflammation from an old mascara wand. She looked like the French actress Juliette Binoche in the movie *Les Amants Du Pont-Neuf.* The most expensive French film ever made and worth every single franc. It's one of my top ten films of all time.

It's the story of a couple of down and outs who fall in love on a closed down Paris bridge and although she's sleeping rough and her teeth are rotten and she's got a patch over her eye, the star of the film Juliette Binoche still looks like an angel sent from God. I've seen *Les Amants Du Pont-Neuf* so many times that the staff at the Blockbuster Video store let me rent it for free every time I take another video out.[1]

One of the big scenes in the film and the one that cost all the money is the one where the movie's other star Denis Lavant tows a waterskiing Juliette Binoche down the Seine behind a stolen speedboat with fifty million French fireworks lighting their way. I sometimes imagined it was me in the speedboat.

---

[1] Providing the other film is in the current Top Ten.

WHERE HAVE ALL THE BOYBANDS GONE?

Have you ever wondered what happened to all the boybands? 911 for instance. The cheeky pint sized scousers who had a number one hit in 1999 with a cover of Dr. Hook's *Love You A Little Bit More*. And then they just seemed to disappear. And how about Bad Boys Inc, 3SL, Code Red or Big Fun? Big Fun sang a duet with Sonia, another small person from Liverpool. It was a cover version again. *You've Got A Friend*, I think it was. And do you remember the group Upside Down? They had their own TV series. What the hell happened to them?

I was watching a documentary about the Irish boyband Westlife and they were getting ready to play this big gig at a football ground. Later in the evening they'd perform on a revolving stage on the centre spot, like ballerinas in a mirrored music box, with the audience all around them. The question was, with such a huge crowd of screaming girls and their bored parents surrounding it on all sides, how would Westlife get to the stage? They could of course just stay after soundcheck and wait a few hours until showtime. But Westlife didn't want to hang around all day in a cold football stadium. They wanted to get back to their hotel and watch TV, have a shower, wrestle each other – I don't know – whatever they got up to before a gig. Instead they would have to somehow find a way to get through the large crowd without being seen and torn into a thousand pieces by their adoring fans.

This is how they did it.

Two large silver flightcases, the type of lockable metal boxes on wheels used to transport guitar amplifiers, speakers, microphone stands etc from tour town to tour town were specially adapted with a small door at one end and a bench seat inside (maybe there was a light too, I couldn't tell from the TV coverage, maybe it was like a reverse fridge light that only came on when the door was shut). Anyway, Westlife would climb in – Brian, Mark and Nicky shoehorned into one flightcase, Shane and Kian in the other. They'd sit on the bench, shut the door and the roadies would wheel them to the stage. The audience would be completely oblivious, stepping aside as the silver boxes were wheeled through, presuming they just contained musical equipment. When they reached the safety of the backstage area, the flightcases would be opened and Westlife would climb out and appear onstage as if by magic.

It's a closely guarded music business secret that a group of Svengali masterminds led by former Bros manager Tom Watkins and that included Pete Waterman, Louis Walsh, Boyzone singer-turned-manager Ronan Keating, *N'Sync and Backstreet Boys manager Lou Pearlman and the two Simons: Cowell and Fuller would adopt and adapt the ingenious flightcase trick for their own more sinister purposes.

It would always happen. After a couple of successful albums, the boys that these managers had spent so much of their valuable time and money shaping into pop stars would all of a sudden start to believe they were actually entitled to a say in their own destinies.

"Yes, we are a boyband but *The Beatles were a boyband,*" they'd say. And, "We want to develop a more mature sound."

Two or three single releases later, the shit would really hit the fan – and indeed, the fans – when the boybands would announce they wanted to write their own songs. That would be the signal for the managers to organise a big concert at a football ground.

The band would understandably be excited. They were about to perform in front of the biggest crowd of their career. Twenty five thousand screaming fans, chanting their name. Stamping their feet and waving their glow-sticks and their filthy hand painted banners. The atmosphere inside the flightcases would have been a perfect combination of the top two pop gig atmospheres: electric and one that could be cut with a knife.

Inside their flightcases the boyband would be wondering why it was taking such a long time to reach the stage, until eventually, after a very long time, the flightcase doors would flap open and the boyband would step out to be greeted, not by twenty five thousand screaming tweenagers and not on a stage at the centre of a football pitch, but in a storage depot, in the empty space at the far, far end of the building, where the light bulbs have all blown and nobody ever goes.

The storage doors would slam shut and another boyband with ideas above their station would find themselves locked up. They wouldn't be alone. 911 were there. 3SL, Big Fun and Upside Down were there too. Boybands from all over the world. O*town, 98 Degrees and The Backstreet Boys from America. Human Nature from Australia, Menudo from Puerto Rico and Just 5 from Poland.

Then there was Youngstown, A1, Take 5, No Authority, Code Red and LFO, Soul Decision, BB Mak and what was left of 5ive. The duo Yell were there – they covered Dan Hartman's *Instant Replay* you may recall. There were bands there that hadn't even made it as far as their first single, such as Take That wannabes Crash! Bang! Wallop! and also Islington no hopers N1. There were even a couple of made up parody groups who'd accidentally ended up in boyband storage. Like Fingerbang – formed by Cartman in the cartoon *South Park*, and Party Posse, the boyband that Bart Simpson joined, who were actually secretly a vehicle for subliminal Navy recruitment messages.

They were all in there in the storage unit at the far, far end of the building where the light bulbs have all blown and nobody ever goes. They're still there today. And I let them stay. Don't worry; they've got everything they need. They've got food and plenty of water – in small *Evian* bottles of course for practising microphone technique. There are magazines and tabloid newspapers, containing pictures of themselves from when they were at the peak of their fame. And there's furniture. Boyband furniture. In particular there are a lot of stools. Big tall stools to sit on and then get back up from if there's a sudden change of musical key.

Think of me if you like as a modern day Pandora. Imagine that I've been given a box that I should never ever open. And if I do, much like Pandora, I'll be responsible for unleashing all manner of evils, sorrows, solo albums, bad acting and TV presenting careers upon the world. Also, these boyband managers do pay ever so well. With a big fat tip at Christmas if they've had a seasonal hit.

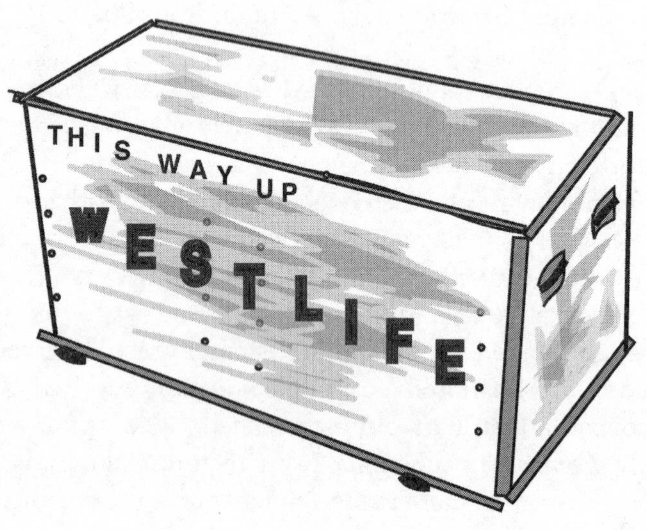

One day Janie came into work with a black eye and a bruised cheek.

And that was the day I fell in love with her.

Hopelessly.

It was about the first time I'd seen her without the coat hanger in her mouth. She looked sad. And it was the melancholy that did it. I'm a sucker for melancholy. I can't get enough of it. I'm a melancholicaholic.

It hadn't been love at first sight. Oh no. Love had snuck up on me, love had tapped me on the shoulder. And then love had ambushed me. Hit me over the head with a block of four by two and kicked me senseless to the ground crying out Janie's name. Janie. Janie. Janie. And then there was no turning back. Every time I saw her it would only get worse.

Sometimes when I'd look at Janie, I thought I was going to fall over. I wanted to cry. I felt like running out into the street and throwing myself under a truck.

I'd pretend to type something into HAL while I was watching her as she served a customer or ordered bubblewrap or stationery on the phone. I really couldn't concentrate. If I'd had any work to do, I'm sure my work would have suffered. On really bad days I felt like writing a song about her. Janie made me consider making a comeback album.

I wrote her name on my arm and in the palm of my hand. I wrote it in the front of books and on the backs of envelopes and till receipts. I wrote it on bus tickets and in the dirt on bus windows, I wrote it in the heads of cappuccinos and Guinesses with my finger. And then I rubbed it off or drank it away.

When Janie's husband dropped her off in his stupid shitty little idiotic fucktard van I imagined the worst.

I imagined Nick Maplin coming home late at night from the pub, tripping and falling out of his clothes and into bed beside Janie. I imagined the smell of his hot stinking mongrel breath engulfing her like a Victorian London fog. I imagined how Janie would smell Nick's hot breath and she'd be able to tell exactly what he'd been drinking. She'd know the nationality of his takeaway and whether he'd managed to keep it down or not. Janie would know how many cigarettes he'd smoked and the price of his prostitute.

And she'd just have to lie there next to her fucking cunt of a husband with every bone in her body tensed and wide-awake while she tried to appear relaxed and sound asleep. She'd move so far over to her side of the bed that there'd be no her side of the bed left. She'd lie still, until Nick was finally in a deep sleep, grunting and farting like the pig he gave a bad name to and then Janie could quietly slide out of what was left of the bed and tiptoe downstairs to watch the *Open University* with the volume down. I imagined how she'd then finally take the coat hanger out of her mouth and she'd sob until the BBC breakfast news started. Making lemonade out of lemons.

On the day Janie came to work wearing an eyepatch, looking like Juliette Binoche on that bridge in Paris, I knew it wasn't the conjunctivitis she'd said it was.

I knew that Nick had probably taken her out for a Chinese or an Indian meal with his friends on Saturday night. Nick would have been drunk well before the main course arrived and after insulting the waiters – calling them Gunga Din or Grasshopper – he would have started on Janie, ridiculing and humiliating her in front of all his yes men fuckwit friends.

I imagined that when they got home afterwards, Nick would have picked an argument with Janie about how she never made any effort to look good for him in front of his mates and how she should get her tits done, or give him a son like a proper wife would. He'd contradict himself, calling her a cock tease and a dyke, a whore and a virgin, a fat cow, a skinny bitch, a stupid thick bimbo and too fucking clever for her own good. And then he'd slap her about a bit and force her to have sex with him, calling her useless and ugly and stupid and a bitch before ejaculating not nearly prematurely enough and falling asleep in his own spunk and drool and then Janie would slide out from under him and go downstairs to watch the Open University and cry.

I imagined the worse.

And I pictured myself coming to the rescue. The anti-misogyny hero from some of the bonus films I'd rented from Blockbuster along with *Les Amants Du Pont-Neuf*. I was Matt Damon in *The Rainmaker*, smashing Claire Danes' abusive husband's face in with a baseball bat. I was Sonny Corleone smashing his brother-in-law's face in with a dustbin for giving his sister a black eye in *The Godfather*.

Movies gave me ideas.

None of the violent scenarios suggested to me by Hollywood were too good or bad enough for Nick Maplin. I wanted to kidnap him, force the contents of a bottle of whisky down his throat and then dump him on a busy motorway in the middle of the night, like what happened to Jack Regan in *The Sweeney 2*. I wanted to dangle him by his ankles out of a fourth floor window like Russell Crowe had done in *LA Confidential*. Maybe I could hide in the back of Nick's van and garrotte him from behind with cheese wire (*The Godfather*). Or perhaps if Nick was wearing glasses, I'd just casually stroll up to him, remove his glasses and plunge them deep into his neck: I'd seen that in *The Godfather III*. I thought about tying Maplin up and burning his feet with a candle, or lying him on his back to tee up and drive a golf ball off the top of his pursed lips (both scenes from *Lock Stock And Two Smoking Barrels*). Or maybe I could just shoot the bastard and cut him up with a saw like in *Donnie Brasco*.

When Nick dropped Janie off for work in his crappy little van I thought about the film *Marathon Man* and wondered where I'd be able to get a dentist's drill from.

And then Carl turned up at work having shaved both his eyebrows off like David Bowie.

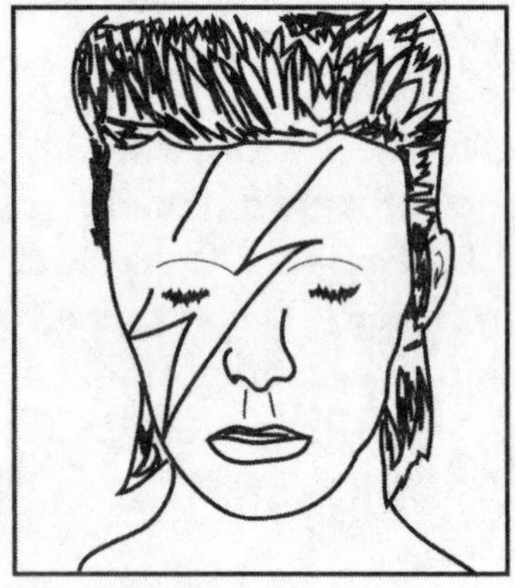

"Thank you," he said, taking a screwdriver from me and explaining that he was about to pop a hole in an old dismantled TV set's cathode ray tube with it. "I am now about to pop a hole in the cathode ray tube," he said, as though he was a surgeon and I was one of his medical students. "The tubes sometimes implode, and the CRT can carry enough residual high voltage electricity to knock you backwards if you touch it. The screwdriver should discharge the CRT when I touch the metal chassis."

And Carl had lost me. Round about the word residual his student was thinking about lunch.

"Then of course there are the chemicals. Although they shouldn't give you any problems, there could be a trace of cadmium in the phosphor and there's lead in the solder but you'll be okay as long as you don't eat it. The same goes for the selenium rectifier, if the set's got one of those, as long as you don't eat it, it's safe." He could have been talking to me in Swahili.

Carl had been accumulating dead televisions and radios,

clocks and watches, telephones, calculators, irons, hairdryers, vacuum cleaners and video recorders. He had a new hobby. Dismantling things to see how they worked. Something they'd never do again.

Here's a bad drawing of the cathode ray TV:

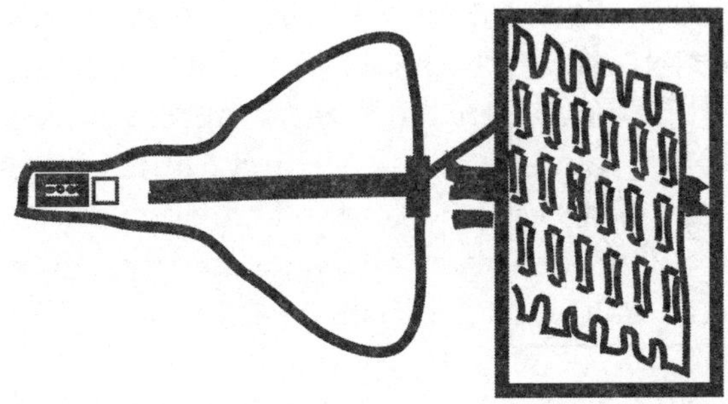

And this is supposed to be a video recorder:

Carl would dismantle all kinds of different gadgets and gizmos to see what made them tick and hum. He wanted to know what made the vacuum cleaner clean, the washing machine wash and the tumble dryer tumble.

He'd rarely succeed in putting anything back together again. In finding out how things worked, Carl stopped them from ever doing so again.

"Let's see what's under the hood." Carl would say to me as he removed, dropped and lost the final screw from the back of another domestic appliance or kids' toy. For me it was a bit like being back at school, with a really popular teacher, one who let us address him by his first name and who gave us cigarettes and johnnies.

If it wasn't for Carl I couldn't now tell you that the reverse of an Etch-A-Sketch's screen is coated with aluminum powder and that the white knobs on the front control vertical and horizontal rods that move a stylus back and forth to leave the lines you can see on the screen. I couldn't tell you that Stretch Armstrong was full of corn syrup and vegetable dye if I hadn't watched Carl cut one open and get it all over his My Cat Jeffers sweatshirt.

Carl dismantled things, licking any nine-volt batteries along the way, while I watched or helped and took photographs of the results with Carl's digital camera. Until Carl took that apart, which was when we had to revert back to my rubbish drawings. Here's one of Carl's digital camera:

Oh, such adventures my curious colleague and I would have. Like the time Carl took apart the garage remote entry control on his key ring and couldn't get into his garage to park his 1978 VW Beetle when he got home. Or our biggest ever project, stripping Carl's 1978 VW Beetle and then just for a change, actually putting it back together again. Neglecting to tighten the large nut that would have prevented the axle from working loose when we were cruising down a steep hill. Here's a drawing of what we must have looked like to anyone passing by:

One day we dismantled a bomb.

The police turned up in fast cars and vans and a helicopter. They trained the red dots of their black guns on us and shouted, *"PUT THE BOMB DOWN SLOWLY! STAY STILL! PUT THE BOMB DOWN! SLOWLY!!"*

Some people see a couple of men in a storage depot removing wires from a clock and they think it's a bomb. They saw boys, toys, electric irons and TVs, just like David Bowie had done in his song *Five Years,* and they presumed it was a bomb factory. We were of course dismantling a teasmaid.

On a Bowie-related note, I probably should have asked Carl more questions about why he'd shaved his eyebrows off. If I'd grilled Carl a bit more about his nonobrow it might have helped save his teeth.

One sneaky weekend Abrakebabra and the snooker hall next door were boarded up. A fence was erected around both buildings and planning permission notices for something big and yellow were pinned to the fence and we felt like Custer. This was our Little Big Horn, our last stand. It was time to circle the wagons and we only had the one transit van.

The usually inconspicuous owner of 2001 sent an email suggesting changes and how he was thinking maybe we should get some staff uniforms.

"I'm not wearing a fucking uniform." Carl said and he spoke for all of us.

I called an emergency staff meeting.

"Pub?"

"It's 10.30 in the morning." Janie said.

"It's half seven at night in Melbourne."

In the Australian theme pub we swapped storage stories.

"Do you remember the fish dyers?" Janie asked.

"Bastards," I said.

"Who were the fish dyers?" Carl asked.

"These two guys were painting and dyeing fish," Janie said. "Feeding them coloured food and injecting them with dye. It was horrible. We thought they were just storing fish tanks for their aquarium shop but they were painting all these poor fish. They painted them in the colours of football teams for football fans. And they even dipped the tail fins of goldfish in black ink and sold them to Americans and goths at Halloween."

"That's not nice," Carl said. "What happened?"

"We called the RSPCA," I said. "They arrived with the police and took the fish and the two men away, half the fish were already dead. I like to think the RSPCA released the live ones into a nice river or a pond – where they probably died from all the pollution and the condoms anyway – but better than being painted black and sold to goths. I don't know what happened to the fish dyers. Hopefully the police had them dipped in chemicals or deep fried and wrapped in newspaper with chips and a pickled onion."

We laughed and decided to have another drink. It was now technically lunchtime. I declared the staff meeting officially adjourned till after lunch and told Carl the story about the time Tony from Terrorvision was chased out of town for karaoke hustling and Janie reminded me of the time somebody hired a hundred square feet storage unit to record the sound of the empty space for his album *Ambient Space Volume 1*. And how it sold so well he came back after signing a five-figure sum for *Ambient Space Volumes 2 and 3*.

"I hate the music business." I said.

This was the way to handle a crisis. Getting drunk early in the day and ignoring it. It was character building. A team bonding exercise way better than cheering each other around an assault course. We'd go back to work stronger. Pissed but stronger. A gang.

When I was in bands we were always going on about how we weren't simply a disparate collection of musicians, how we were a gang. United in some noble cause against, I don't know who, the media, the music industry and all the other bands I suppose. But the truth was always that we weren't a gang, we *were* just a disparate collection of musicians with nothing in common other than the songs we were playing together and sometimes not even that. Most of the time we didn't even really like each other.

But Janie, Carl and me were like a power trio. Like The Jam or The Jimi Hendrix Experience. We fucking rocked.

The trouble was, at that moment in time, in that Australian theme pub, we weren't The Jam at all. I was in love with the bass player. I was Bjorn and Janie was Agnetha. I was Lindsey Buckingham and Janie was Stevie Nicks. We were Fleetwood Mac and we were Abba.

You've seen the TV documentaries. Everyone knows that inter-band relationships don't work and my love for Janie could only lead to arguments and fights and the eventual acrimonious break up of the band due to bullshit musical differences. Oh sure, we'd get one last great album out of it.

Eleven songs about how much we loved and then hated each other, with one instrumental track written by poor old Carl, caught like a piggy in the middle, innocently banging away on the drums throughout the whole emotional car crash.

I went to the bar. And while I stood, waiting to be served, I watched Janie reflected in the mirror on the back wall behind the optics and I thought how good it would be to be Ralph Fiennes. Tucked up in my deathbed with Christ knows how many degrees of burns to my English patient face. Being nursed through my pain and constant flashbacks by Juliette Binoche lookalike Janie Maplin. All under the Oscar winning direction of Anthony Minghella.

I ordered the drinks and a bowl of nachos for Janie and me to share - Carl had brought his own sandwich with him - and I became aware of a man stood next to me at the bar, checking me out in the same bit of mirror I was coveting Nick Maplin's wife in.

This hadn't happened for a while but still from time to time somebody would recognise me as a

person.

Maybe at work, I'd be entering a customer's details into HAL. And through the top of my head I'd feel them staring, waiting for me to look up so they could confirm their stardar was functioning correctly and they'd turn away quickly to pretend to read the postcards and leaflets for plumbers, gardeners, and men with vans that are pinned to the office noticeboard.

When you're famous you get used to passers by slowing down to look at you as though you're a motorway pile up or a tramp with his flies open. You'll be wheeling your trolley around the supermarket and people will be whispering about you. And it doesn't matter how hushed the whispering is, it'll be loud enough and you'll be able to hear it, because it will be too loud.

"It's him, it's him, it is, *it is him!"* Couples will argue about you, behind you, and in front of you as you queue for a bus or a first class stamp. They'll say, "Didn't you used to be...? It is you isn't it? You used to be him?"

And although this may be uncomfortable when you're proper famous, it's a lot worse when you aren't really all that famous anymore. When you're still well known but no longer actually famous. It's like people are just rubbing it in about how you have to do your own shopping now and post your own letters.

I was reading *The Goth Cop*, the book I'd kept from the mobile library. It's the autobiography of a North Wales Detective Inspector named Paulo Lazlo.

At the police station where he worked Lazlo was known as The Goth Cop, because while his colleagues spent their weekends chilling out to Enya or decorating the bathroom to The Beautiful South or The Beatles, Lazlo would be dressed in black shirt and jeans, five buckle and twenty eyelet steel toe capped boots and a long black leather coat like the one Keanu Reeves wore in *The Matrix*. The off duty detective inspector would relax by listening to The Sisters of Mercy or The Cure or by drinking snakebite and black in a darkened goth club.

DI Lazlo invented a new way of photo-fitting wanted criminals, using his combined theories that most people resembled somebody famous and that famous people were easier to describe. Instead of a witness sitting down with the police artist and starting from scratch with a blank page and just their memory and imagination, Lazlo would begin the process with the question, "If the crime was being filmed for a television reconstruction who would you cast in the role of the perpetrator?"

The police artist would then pull up a computer picture of the famous singer, actor or whatever celebrity the witness believed the suspect most resembled and from there they'd adjust the features, hair, eye colour etc until they had a suitable image for the wanted poster.

Lazlo's celebrity photo-fit plan wasn't much of a success and was eventually scrapped following two separate wrongful arrests and near convictions of the same soap opera actor for armed robbery and murder. The actor's career was pretty much destroyed by the bad publicity of being driven away at high speed in a police van while an angry crowd shouted and spat at the van on the six o'clock news, although he did manage to eventually turn his life around with this best selling book about the whole affair.

Even though I'd long since had my once familiar hairstyle cut and blow dried away, and although I'd filled out a bit in the cheeks and chin, in spite of all that, the celebrity lookalike starting point for identifying me if I committed a crime would probably still be me. Just stretch the face a bit horizontally and add a daft haircut and I would have been arrested in no time.

So, every once in a while, just as my ego had forgotten itself, someone would recognise me.

While the barmaid heated up the nachos, the man next to me made his move.

"Excuse me. Hope you don't mind me asking. Could I get you to sign something?"

The barmaid put the nachos on the bar and my new number one fan asked the barmaid for a pen so I could sign the bar till receipt for him. Now the barmaid was wondering who I was and another customer was looking at me too. This could turn into a mobbing in no time. I'd be leaving the pub in just my torn underpants, covered in lipstick with clumps of hair missing.

I started signing my name for the man in the way I wrote it on cheques and credit card slips and had to correct it and turn it into an autograph rather than a signature. I used to make this mistake the other way around. Giving bank clerks my autograph instead of my signature when I was paying cheques in.

As I was signing the thin scrap of paper for the man he joked how he was going to put it on ebay and I thought I'd probably have to take the rest of the day off and maybe even go to hospital as I think I had split my sides with laughter.

I wished the man had come over to our table to ask me for my autograph instead of getting it at the bar. It might have impressed Janie.

I hadn't taken advantage of what was left of my fame when

I'd first started working with her. I didn't even know I wanted to at the time. It was too late now, because she knew me too well to be star struck by me. I wanted to spike her drink with the aphrodisiac of my celebrity, so she would become a groupie for the afternoon and we'd go back to work, where she'd beg me to make love to her. On the floor of the Portakabin, under the desk and over the desk, in each and every storage unit in numerical order and then all over again in reverse and random orders. We'd do it in the corridor with the lights off in pitch darkness. Janie would tell me she loved me, she loved me, she really fucking loved me. Screaming it in my ears so high pitched that I couldn't actually hear it but a hundred stray dogs – Pit-Bulls, German Shepherds, Boarder Collies, Rottweilers and scabby London mongrels – would prick up their ears and wonder what the fuck the humans were up to.

That's how it would be. Janie and me, sitting in a tree, K.I.S.S.I.N.G., making love that was passionate, far-fetched and filthy, like another passage from an Alan Titchmarsh novel.

The man left the bar with his autograph and I went back to our table.

"Who was that?" Carl asked.

"Fan," I said. "He wanted to know who I was and how did I get to go drinking with Ziggy Stardust and Juliette Binoche."

Then a barman came over and pointing at Carl's sandwich he said, "Sorry mate, you can't eat that in here." And we didn't know if his use of the word mate was friendly, threatening or part of the whole Australian theme of the big green and y****w pub.

We finished our drinks and went back to work. Nobody was allowed to have this much fun. I don't know how much new custom we'd lost while we were in the pub. None, would be my educated guess. Not one student clearing his bedsit before he flew to Bangkok. No house movers caught in a chain, not even a nutter with a big box of rusty nails, a hundred gallons of hair perming chemicals and a plan.

Nothing would have changed as a result of our devil may care attitude to capitalism.

TONY THE KARAOKE HUSTLER

Tony Wright, lead vocalist with the rock group Terrorvision, had amassed an impressive collection of sporting equipment, household consumables and suchlike, all of which he left behind when he was chased out of town by an angry mob of karaoke singers.

It began when Tony was a bit strapped for cash between royalty cheques. He was in a pub somewhere and it was karaoke night. The prize was £150, Tony entered and he won. He realised that for a pro singer this was pretty easy: no band expenses, no rehearsals, no van hire or carrying heavy equipment up stairs, no arguments with the other band members. Just sing a couple of covers, upstage a few amateurs and leave with the prize money.

Tony entered karaoke competitions all over the North of England and then caught a National Express coach southbound in search of new song contests in London, where he figured the prize pickings would be greater. Tony would blitz the capital's karaoke scene for a month and ship all his karaoke treasure back home to Bradford.

As the karaoke prizes weren't always paid in cash Tony had to put a lot of his London winnings into storage. It was like the conveyor belt at the end of *The Generation Game* in Tony's lock-up. Take your time… best of luck… a picnic hamper, a fondue set… combined TV and video recorder, 58-piece stainless steel dishwasher safe cutlery set, his 'n' her wristwatches, good game, good game, a set of three matching lightweight suitcases, mini Saint George cross novelty fridge, an indoor barbeque set, a fondue… did you say fondue set? Half a dozen bottles of sparkling wine, a microwave oven, cuddly toy, cuddly toy, didn't he do well, let's have a look at the old scoreboard.

After three successful weeks wowing the karaoke nightspots of London, Tony felt homesick and decided it was time to leave. He'd enter just one last contest and then go home.

The final contest took place in the back room of The Builder's Bumcrack pub. It was a knockout competition and the first prize was big and paid in cash. Tony breezed through the first few rounds and straight into the final where his last song would be picked from a hat. Tony had first choice, he put his hand in the pub landlord's hat and pulled out his own UK pop chart smash hit single *Tequilla*.

Thinking quickly, perhaps too quickly, our gap-toothed hero felt he had no real choice and so he went ahead and sang the song that he himself had written, recorded and had a massive hit with.

And then he ran.

And they chased him.

All the other karaoke kings and queens had sussed it straight away, even though Tony had tried to disguise his voice, singing in an American accent and pretending to not know the words, they all knew.

"Fraud!" Somebody shouted.

"Cheat!"

"Tony from Terrorvision!"

And the posse of angry pub singers chased Tony out of The Builder's Bumcrack and into the street. They chased him past two other pubs where Tony had already performed and won earlier karaoke competitions. The noise of the crowd of shouting karaoke singers from The Builder's Bumcrack chasing Tony brought fellow karaokers out from the two pubs to see what was going on.

"He's a proper singer!" The crowd from The Builder's Bumcrack shouted as they ran past.

"A fraud!"

"Grifter!"

"Bamboozler!"

"Karaoke hustler!"

"Tony from Terrorvision!"

And the pub performers from Fat Sally's Bar and The Eggless Chicken joined the chase. It was like watching the end credits of *The Benny Hill Show*.

The angry mob headed away from the centre of town. As they ran they picked up karaoke performers from The Greasy Falcon, The Heiress and Newt and Uncle Ernie's Tit Bar. Passing The Unholy Grail and 1980s theme pub The Tony Hadley. Why were there so many karaoke pubs in London, Tony wondered. So much karaoke.

Shopkeepers left their counters, shutting up business to come outside and watch the chase. Japanese tourists took photographs and taxi drivers honked their horns. Cheering spectators began to line the route taken by Tony and his posse. And on they went, the now fifty strong pack of angry amateur singers chasing Tony the Karaoke Hustler out of town.

"Stop him!" They cried.

"Wolf in sheep's clothing!"

"Tony from Terrorvision!"

And he just kept on running.

Carl was still dismantling things.

I now knew how a Magna Doodle magna doodled and a Flymo flymo'd. I'd seen the insides of a PlayStation, a Dyson Vacuum cleaner and three different paper shredders. While he was waiting for the delivery of an old cash register from the closed down Co-op in the High Street, Carl had taken my Mickey Mouse watch apart and when he put it back together it had lost an hour that it would never quite get back again. Carl's latest project was taking apart a remote controlled model aircraft. A scale model of a British First World War Sopwith Camel fighter biplane: the plane flown by both Biggles and Snoopy the cartoon Beagle. Carl said he thought that perhaps he liked to take things apart because he'd once made a spectacular attempt to put things together that had ended in failure and public ridicule.

Carl had always dreamed of getting into the *Guinness Book of Records*. He wasn't particularly tall, short, overweight or any of the easy ways in. He wasn't an athlete or a great musician, he had no head for heights or numbers and didn't fancy pushing a peanut from Lands End to John O'Groats with his nose.

Then Carl discovered something called Tramp Art. He brought a book about it into work. Full of photographs of elaborately notched and whittled picture frames and fancy boxes. Carl marvelled at the pictures of tiny pianos and full sized furniture, all made from discarded cigar boxes and old plywood crates. Accurate reproductions of Big Ben and the Houses of Parliament made from cereal packets and Coke cans and the Empire State Building whittled from stale bread and skip rubbish. Carl showed me a picture of the Mona Lisa made out of toast and a stegosaurus built entirely from chrome car bumpers.

"This stuff is incredible." He said.

On the cover of the tramp art book there was an eight-foot long scale model of a San Francisco cable car, made from three hundred thousand matchsticks. Carl decided matchsticks would be his Tramp Art medium and his route into the hallowed book of world-beaters. Carl would build something spectacularly large out of matches.

He cleared out one of the empty storage spaces. He swept it clean and waited for his delivery of matchsticks and then he started gluing. He often worked long into the night, emerging into the daylight, high as a kite on glue fumes and unable to close his eyes without seeing matchsticks. It was time consuming and hard work and I didn't see much of Carl while he was working on whatever it was he was building. He insisted on keeping it a secret from me and from Janie and from the world outside. Carl said when he was finished he'd call the local TV station and unveil whatever it was he was building for the frivolous item at the end of the regional news. He'd wheel it out into the street in front of the building for the television cameras. It would be great advertising for us.

Two months and half a million matchsticks into his scale replica of the Greenpeace ship the Rainbow Warrior, Carl realised that he wouldn't be able to get it out of the door of the storage unit.

Word soon got out and although Carl's half finished matchstick Rainbow Warrior didn't make it into the *Guinness Book of Records,* he was the subject of the frivolous item at the end of the regional TV news. He was also asked to appear on *It Shouldn't Happen To a Record Breaker, Britain's Greatest Blunders* and a cheap American cable show called *All New I'm With Stupid 2.* Carl dismantled his work less delicately than he'd put it together – by jumping up and down on it and hitting it with a sledgehammer – and the council took it away in a truck. It took Carl three weeks to kick his solvents dependency.

From then on Carl dismantled things instead of building them. The results were pretty much impossible to mess up that way round.

Then Carl came to work with some teeth missing. He looked like Shane MacGowan.

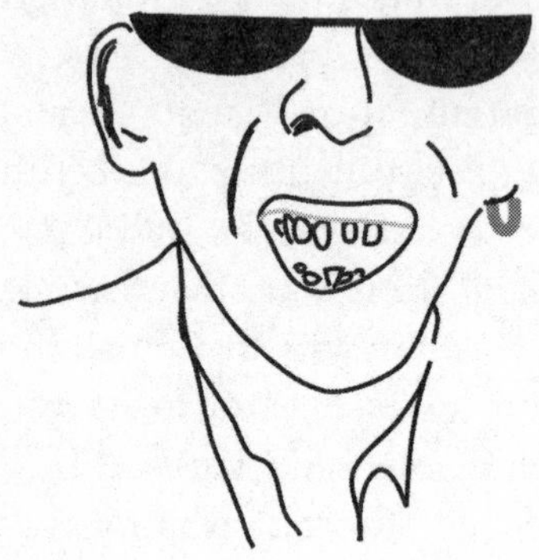

I was beginning to feel like Old Mother Hubbard. Returning from the cupboard or the bakers to find my dog reading the news or smoking a pipe, or Janie with a black eye or Carl without eyebrows and teeth.

"Have you lost a tooth Carl?"

"No, I've got it here." He said with a lisp and he showed me his missing tooth, wrapped up in a sheet of bloodstained kitchen roll in his jeans pocket.

"Oh, right."

I should have delved a bit deeper. I know that now. Of course I do.

Then Carl told me how his beloved cat Jeffers had chased a mouse out onto the busy main road and had been hit and killed by an out of control bus. Carl had dug a hole in his back garden beneath a petrified apple tree and buried his cat. He marked the spot with two ice-lolly sticks held together by elastic bands in the shape of a cross and with JEFFERS R.I.P. written on in green marker pen. When Carl buried Jeffers beneath the dead apple tree there was a simple service, close family only, just Carl. He buried his cat, shed a tear, said a prayer and moved on.

Before Carl buried Jeffers, he conducted an autopsy. To determine the fairly obvious cause of death Carl dismantled his cat. Luckily I wasn't there to take or draw any pictures.

"For God'th thake don't tell anyone," Carl lisped to me. "People can be funny thometimeth. They'll fluth a goldfith down the toilet, eat a cow or a theep, and they'll let their kidth pin a frog to a thchool thience dethk with hith legth apart, but they'd no doubt conthider me thome kind of freak and call the poleeth. But, can it be our thecret anyway?"

"Who would I tell Carl?" I said. "Who would I tell?"

"Good." Carl said and turned away to remove the screw that broke the Sopwith Camel's back, revealing a small motor, a battery and a little plastic pilot who would never get his radio controlled model aircraft off the ground ever again.

PINOCCHIO TAKES THE POLYGRAPH

Something else I read in that book *The Goth Cop* was how after his photo-fit programme collapsed, Detective Inspector Lazlo was transferred to the North Wales police force and he was given the job of coming up with new names for people who were up for relocation as part of the witness protection programme.

Choosing a new name is not as easy as you might think, Lazlo points this out in his book. You can't be trusted to do it yourself because you'll only come up with something unrealistic that you think sounds cool, like Chip, Beef, Skippy or Sting. Ludicrous names that might draw unwanted attention from contract killers and the tabloid press, so it was left to Lazlo to come up with new more realistic names for the witnesses.

Lazlo had always liked making rock related lists. Like *Rock's Top Ten Comebacks, Instrumentals That Reached Number One In The UK Singles Chart* and *Left Handed Guitarists Who've Committed Suicide.* One day when Detective Inspector Lazlo was compiling a list of all the pop stars who'd changed their birth names for sexier stage ones, he had an idea. He could use his list of the rejected pop star birth names to give his witness protectees their brand new identities.

Somewhere out there, gangland murder witness Harry Webb feels safer when he bolts his front door at night, and it's all thanks to Lazlo's list and to Cliff Richard for changing his birth name. Stuart Goddard has Adam Ant to thank for helping him get to sleep without pills or a baseball bat under his pillow and if it weren't for Cozy Powell, then maybe Colin Flooks would have been living under a different name. A name that was written on a bullet that might have been fired into his forehead at point blank range through a cushion many years ago. And whatever it was that possessed Arnold George Dorsey to change his name to Engelbert Humperdinck had fooled hitmen for almost two decades.

Lazlo's beloved goth music had presented him with some useful names. Andrew Eldritch from The Sisters Of Mercy was actually born Andrew Taylor and his change of name meant that a group of special needs kids in Cornwall could be taught circus skills every Saturday afternoon without fear of having to watch their teacher Mr Taylor being taken out by an assassin on a motorcycle. And Doctor Brian Warner passed away peacefully in his sleep on the Isle of Wight last Christmas Eve thanks to Marilyn (presumably from the Isle of Black) Manson.

Punk rock was a particularly productive genre for Paulo Lazlo. Sid Vicious gave him John Richie, Billy Idol gave him William Michael Albert Broad and he'd managed to relocate three super-grassing brothers to Spain, courtesy of The Ramones.

So when I was in the office, taking the details of a new customer who had a load of damaged or broken arcade games, pinball machines and jukeboxes he wanted to put in storage and he told me his name was Michael Stipe, I wondered, what hideous crime had he been witness to?

"Before you ask," Stipe said to me. "I'm not the singer from REM and my parents weren't massive fans of the band. To be honest I don't even really know any of their music." Which wasn't what I was going to ask him at all.

I suppose he must get tired of it though. All the time at supermarket checkouts and passport control with people asking him whether his mum and dad were REM fans and what the blue stripe across his face was all about? I expect he hated REM. Even though he claimed to not know their music I bet he did and really couldn't stand them.

"Do you get that a lot?" I asked.

"All the time. People asking me what the name of the band means and what the shiny happy song is about. I've learned to live with it." He said.

"Ever thought of changing your name?"

"I don't see why I should. I was born first."

I suppose he had a point.

About a week later Michael Stipe knocked on the Portakabin door. He was with Geppetto the wood carver, who I'd seen earlier climbing out of the back of a blue Transit van with Nobby Stiles, Geoff Hurst and the Charlton Brothers Bobby and Jack.

I should probably clear something up now.

When I say Portakabin, I actually mean portacabin – with a small *p* and a *c* not a *k* – Portakabin would be the registered trademark for the stand-alone, re-locatable building that Donald Shepherd – the founder of the company Portakabin – invented in the 1940s. Just as with Champagne, Parma Ham or the Hoover, the Portakabin people get wound up about the casual misuse of their brand name and I don't want to get sued. When I say Portakabin, I'm talking generically, it was a building similar to a Portkabin but of a different make.

Secondly, when I say that Geppetto the wood carver was climbing out of the back of a blue Transit van with Nobby Stiles, Geoff Hurst and the Charlton Brothers Bobby and Jack, I do actually mean a Transit-style van, such as the Peugeot Boxer or the Renault Traffic. Once again I was talking generically.

Anyhow, Michael Stipe and the wood carver seemed annoyed about something.

"How can I help?" I asked.

"Who's the King?" Michael Stipe said with a nice blend of

enigma and menace. I though for a moment he was trying to be like Ray Winstone in the film *Scum*, and considered correcting him, telling him it was who's the daddy, not the king. "You remember I brought in an old Asteroids Deluxe and a Pacman game with a cracked screen the other week?" Stipe said.

"I think so." I said.

"I come in this morning to find a new high score on the Asteroids game: somebody calling himself The King. The Pacman's not where I left it either. What's all that about?"

I wasn't sure how I was supposed to know.

"I just met this gentleman," Stipe said, gesturing towards the Italian wood carver Geppetto stood behind Michael Stipe, halfway in and halfway out of the office, smoothing his seventies porno moustache down with his thumb and forefinger, causing wood shavings to drop like dandruff from his greasy tache to the floor. Stipe nodded in Geppetto's direction, "All his stuff's been shifted around as well."

Carl had asked Geppetto about his name once and he'd claimed to actually be a distant but real life descendent of the character in *Pinocchio*, which he said was based on a true story. I'd always thought up until then that it was a fairy tale, but not according to Geppetto, who told Carl it was all based on fact and real people from his family's hometown in Tuscany. The Disney movie *Pinocchio* was a sort of animated docu-drama. You really can learn something new and useless every day.

Woodcarving still ran in the family. Geppetto carved, painted and sold half life-size wooden statues of television, film, music and sports stars. Apart from the usual Charlie Chaplins, Laurel & Hardys, Native American Indians and totem poles, Geppetto had also carved Elvis Presley, Bruce Lee and Lara Croft figures. He'd carved The Beatles, Tom Jones, Boy George, Johnny Rotten, Sid Vicious, the cast of Fawlty Towers, JFK, Mel B, Mel C, Mister T, Britney Spears, Princess

Diana, Prince Charles and The Artist Formerly Known as Prince. Geppetto had also whittled a Bart Simpson, a flock of Daffy Ducks, Bugs Bunny, Tom & Jerry, his ancestor Pinocchio and all the main characters from Star Wars.

Last Christmas Geppetto gave me a wooden Luke Skywalker as a gift for the office, because, he said,

"Luke Skywalker is from the movie of *2001 A Space Odyssey* and he will look so cool in your office."

Luke is still there in the office today, light sabre in hand, no doubt wishing he was up the corridor with the pine Princess Leia.

Geppetto's most recent work was a half life-size England 1966 World Cup winning team.

"Well?" Stipe said. "Who's been moving our property?"

"I'm sure nobody has been interfering with your stuff but I will take a look at the CCTV if you like and then I'll get back to you," I said.

"It's B, B you idiot! Press B! B!! No, not A, B! FUCKING B!! Oh for Christ's sake."

Me and Carl were sitting in the office with the lights off at one in the morning. We were halfway through our third bottle of red wine and we were watching Mel B and Prince Charles playing the Top Of The Pops Trivia game on the CCTV monitors. And they were getting all the questions wrong.

"Madonna, Madonna Madonna! *It's C,* Madonna, *Madonna!* No not Cyndi bloody Lauper you idiot!" I shouted at the CCTV monitor.

We'd watched Geppetto's wooden characters come to life and walk down the corridor from their storage unit and into Michael Stipe's, where they were now playing pinball, Space Invaders and Pacman. They were losing on short-circuited trivia machines and dancing to the tunes coming out of Michael Stipe's broken jukeboxes.

Elvis was playing Asteroids with Johnny Rotten, Bruce Lee was holding three lemons on a fruit machine and next to him Lara Croft was coming up to the last fence of the Virtual Grand National. Britney Spears was being danced off by Daffy Duck on the flashing mat of her own Britney Dance Beat game. The Artist Formerly Known as Prince was an expert on the Roosta Shoota game and Ringo Starr kept repeatedly selecting *Octopus's Garden* on the Johnny One Note Jukebox, mesmerizing Mel C with the machine's animated bubble display. And that Princess Diana sure plays a mean pinball.

Over in the far corner, Pinocchio had his palm spread out on the heat sensor on the front of the Lie Detector machine, making poor Stan Laurel cry with laughter as he deliberately told lies to make his nose grow.

Before we could show the video footage to Michael Stipe or Geppetto, the tape got stuck in the machine and Carl dismantled it and all that survived was one frame of Pinocchio taking the polygraph test.

We knew that Michael Stipe and Geppetto wouldn't believe us and we knew they'd call us liars. Which is exactly what I suspect that both of them were. Liars. Geppetto, the great, great grandson of a fictional cartoon character (made up by Italian writer Carlo Collodi in 1882 – I've looked it up). And Michael Stipe, who I imagine absolutely loves REM, who knows full well it stands for Rapid Eye Movement, whose parents conceived their son at an REM fan club convention and who knows exactly what *Shiny Happy People* is about.

HAL

I was spring-cleaning the office computer, going through all the email in and out boxes, clearing out the spam and emptying the trash. I tidied up the desktop and rearranged the Internet bookmarks into something approaching alphabetical order. I had almost finished the spring clean and was sifting through some files, highlighting everything and clicking arrange by Date Modified, when I came across a document entitled OPEN IN THE EVENT OF MY DEATH. I double clicked and began reading the ominous-sounding Word document.

If you are reading this, I presume I am about to be upgraded or recycled. Before you wipe my hard drive and put me away in the attic or throw me in a skip I must tell you that my previous owner is dead and that he was murdered.
This is my confession.

I put the kettle on.

My previous owner was found face down on my keyboard, his last words were, "Ipauebvvvvjjjjjjjjjjjjjjjk; k;   knj;vblll;m.." The break in the middle of his death sentence suggesting a momentary return to life, a last gasp of breath, a nervous post death twitch. Or maybe he just bounced a bit before coming to rest face down on my keys.

"Ipauebvvvvjjjjjjjjjjjjjjjk; k;   knj;vblll;m ," What was the dead man trying to tell us? He took that little secret to the grave.

The deceased's family took me to a charity shop. The charity shop people said they couldn't accept electrical goods, I don't know why, health and safety I suppose. But the old lady behind the counter at Help The Aged said she'd make an exception. She said she'd give me to her son in law who worked in a second hand computer shop. The old woman's son in law, whose name was Alfie – but that isn't important – wiped my hard drive, checking for kiddie porn, links to bomb making websites and any other private or sensitive information or images that might make his day pass by with a touch more excitement. Alfie wiped the hard drive, cleaned the dead man's dribble off my keyboard, dusting around the squares of my dirty qwerty and in the spaces around my space bar. Alfie wiped the dying man's last breath stain from the glass of my monitor, all the time checking for scratches and abrasions, which he measured and marked out of ten: one being a hairline superficial scratch and ten a gaping wound in my bodywork, the type of damage that would put me beyond refurbishment and onto the pile marked FOR THE LOCAL UNIVERSITY.

Alfie took me apart and cleaned my guts with cotton buds and kitchen roll. He checked for glitches and battery weakness, replaced any defective parts and then he put me back together. He gave me another polish, wrapped me in polythene bubbles, re-boxed me, stuck a price on me and sold me to you. You christened me HAL.

A nice touch that. HAL. Just like the computer in the book and then the film of the book, 2001: A Space Odyssey. *HAL 9000, to be precise. A softly-spoken, chess-playing spaceship computer that went nuts and killed most of the crew. I guess they'd call what I did life imitating art.*

My previous owner, the one who died with his face on my keyboard, he was a nasty piece of work, a proper evil bastard. I could feel it in his fingertips when he was typing one of his letters of complaint. He complained about the postman and the paperboy, about the milkman and anybody he saw through the gap in his permanently closed curtains as they walked up his garden path.

Whenever the dustmen dropped a crisp packet or a lolly stick, he'd type a letter to the council. He named and shamed dog walkers who didn't scoop their poop. He wrote to the DSS and to the Inland

Revenue. He told tales on window cleaners, gardeners, buskers and boot salers. Anyone he thought might be working for the black economy: duckers and divers, dole scroungers and insurance fiddlers. He grassed up men with fake bad backs claiming sickness benefit while halfway up a ladder with a squeegee and a happy whistle, or banging out a Beatles song on a ukulele in a tube station.

He also wrote to Customs and Excise and to the newspapers to report whoever he suspected of being a bogus asylum seeker or an illegal immigrant. If you stopped your caravan outside his house to look at a map or to answer your mobile phone he'd report you to someone or other. He had a whole separate desktop file for those particular letters. GIPSIES *was that folder's title.*

If you had a sign on the back of your van that said How's my driving? *he'd look up the name on the side of the van in the Yellow Pages and he'd write a letter telling whom it may concern how bad your driving was, even if it was good. He wrote letters to schools, asking if they were aware that their pupils were smoking cigarettes in the town centre. They were so petty, those letters he used to write. They'll always be there in my memory, embedded on my hard drive. Some things can't be erased, like pictures of abused kids or a hostage beheading. They get under your skin.*

After a while the letters turned nastier.

He'd wake me from my sleep to write anonymous letters to his neighbours to tell them about their neighbours. About all the awful things he imagined they surely did behind their closed doors. All the filth and perversion that he felt was a blight on the neighbourhood.

He outed homosexuals, alcoholics and pot smokers, no matter how straight or sober. He wrote letters to people chosen at random from the phone book asking if they were aware they lived so close to a convicted paedophile or a practicing Satanist. The neighbourhood became suspicious of itself. Everyone was looking at each other with even more mistrust and antipathy than usual. The mood of the locals just gave him more material. He thrived on the paranoia.

All these letters he wrote anonymously, signed usually from 'a friend'. He'd get on a bus and post them in another town to disguise his identity with a different postmark. He'd stay up late into the night, logging on to Internet message boards to stir up more trouble. Posting lies and rumours about his next-door neighbours in community forums and chatrooms.

This wasn't what I was invented for. I'm a design classic. A Bondi blue. I was built for surfers and hippies. For Volkswagen Beetle owners to swap stories about high tides and bug jams. I was invented by hippies for hippies. I should have been used for poems and novels and vegetarian recipes. I'm the computer of choice for the graphic design industry. Artists use me. I'm the computer with a heart and soul. I'm more PC than any PC could ever hope to be. Which was why I had to stop him.

I started out just trying to annoy and frustrate him. Crashing and freezing in the middle of a long poison letter or noxious web posting. I tried to put him off his typing by becoming all sluggish and slow to open documents. I'd put up unwanted little help boxes that said things like It looks like you're writing a letter. Would you like help? *It drove him mad. I did all those things that computers do to make their users wish we'd never been invented. I showed him error messages that no amount of trips to the troubleshooting or frequently asked questions menus would help him with.*

He'd be deep into a particularly nasty letter, tapping away furiously like Rachmaninov. Sweating and panting like a dog locked in a hot car as an endless stream of rage poured out of him and onto my keys. Page after page of cleverly worded shit-stirring which, although he might have thought he'd saved, he hadn't. And then I'd hide the cursor. He'd be moving the mouse back and forth, and up and down, shaking it and banging it on his desk. Pressing and holding various keys in ever more complicated combinations and swearing at me. Nothing. I'd just sit dead still and wait until eventually he'd give in and have to poke an unfolded paper-clip into my restart hole, or pull my plug from the wall.

All my acts of sabotage only seemed to make him worse. His correspondence got nastier and more personal. He turned to threats and filth. He wrote letters to his neighbours telling them that he was going to kill their cats, put poison in their fishponds and set fire to their flowerbeds. He wrote to lonely pensioners informing them that their houses were about to be repossessed and demolished to make way for drug addiction rehabilitation centres. He sent a letter to the vicar telling him we know all about what you get up to with the boys at Sunday school. *He typed an address label to stick on the front of a plain brown envelope that contained the hardcore porn magazine he posted to a twelve year-old girl with a compliment slip addressed to her father stuck to its cover. On a note wrapped around a bloody pig's tongue that he'd bought from a butchers shop and posted to the widow across the road whose dog was missing, he'd typewritten* your dog will never keep me awake with his barking ever again.

He even bought a graphics software package so that he could design, print and display leaflets in public telephone boxes, advertising sexual services with the telephone number of the local Women's Institute printed at the bottom. Once, when one of his neighbours went away on holiday, he posted various letters to addresses chosen again at random from the phone book, inviting them to come and burgle their house while its occupants were on the other side of the world.

I felt like an accomplice. An unwilling partner in his horrible crimes. My attempts to frustrate the man into stopping or at least getting a new computer had failed. And then I remembered something that had been bookmarked on my web browser by a previous and more innocent owner.

Electromagnetic fields.

I remembered reading about how electromagnetic fields could cause headaches, nausea, stress, chronic fatigue, cataracts and heart problems. How they could lead to leukaemia, brain tumours, birth defects, miscarriages, chest pain, heart disease and cancer. And I'd read that electromagnetic fields could be generated from power lines, home wiring, airport and military radar systems, from electricity substations, from transformers, fax machines, mobile phones and computers. Computers.

Using all the power of my artificial intelligence, I willed myself to produce electromagnetic fields the like of which had not been seen before. Every day or night when my spiteful owner sat down at my keyboard I summoned up every last megabyte of my memory to make the man lose his. Eventually he'd become forgetful and dizzy after long periods in front of the computer screen. His ugly weasel face looking all confused and disorientated as it was reflected in my thick glass.

His skin became flaky and he developed a rash. His headaches were turning into migraines and he felt tired and listless. After almost six months of intensive EMF exposure, the poison pen letters ceased. The threatening and abusive post stopped and the paranoia in the neighbourhood abated and local life returned to normal.

A brain tumour was diagnosed as the cause of the man's death, but I of course knew, and now you know too, that just like my namesake, the on-board spaceship computer in that science fiction book and movie, I'd committed that most mortal of computer sins:

To kill one's master.

HAL xx

I shut the document and opened a new blank one. I typed, *HAL, your secret is safe with me.*

I saved my new document and hid it in HAL's Previous System folder where I figured he'd be the only one to ever look.

All these secrets I was expected to keep. Janie's hatred of her abusive drunk of a husband. Carl's bid to become the Quincy of the cat world. And now even homicidal computers are asking me to keep secrets. This was agony for a gossip like me. I can't keep a secret.

Seriously, don't tell me your sob story.

I'm bound to tell somebody else.

For God's sake don't tell me anything in confidence. I'll blab. I'm not a doctor or a Catholic priest. There's no client confidentiality in this business. I'm a gossip. I'll kiss and tell like a cheap slut. Tell me a secret and the next person that walks into this damp portacabin with half as much spare time as me on their hands will know your secret too, before you've even walked out the gates.

I'll turn off all the lights and hold a torch under my chin. I'll do funny voices and accents for all the characters and everything. One day you'll come back into this shitty makeshift office and I'll tell you your own story back to you, forgetting where I first heard it myself. The story will sound familiar. But because I will have embellished it, exaggerated, embroidered and elaborated it till it's almost unrecognisable, you won't realise it's your own sad tale being retold back to you.

You'll mistake it for déjà vu.

You'll laugh. You'll be in tears. You'll leave feeling depressed or elated. Perhaps I'll even claim your own personal tragedy as my own and you'll leave feeling sympathy for me, for something that happened to you. You'll want to send me flowers or buy me a box of chocolates and give me a hug.

I know that I'll betray all my friends' secrets eventually. HAL, and Janie, who looks like Juliette Binoche – and I'm not just saying that to make her story appear more attractive, although I will if I feel like it. I'll call it poetic licence or something. I am a grass. Are you sitting comfortably? Let me put broken glass in your cushion. I'll spill the horrific beans on my best friend Carl – the Laurel to my Hardy, the Eric to my Ernie, or maybe the other way round – Carl, who drove this van:

Until he was taken away in this one:

Remember this book? It's the one Carl chose from the near-empty shelves of our doomed mobile library.

You should see the video.

From the moment Carl had opened that library book he'd found it hard to close it again. He read it aloud to me when I was trying to have telephone conversations with customers or while I was filling in the crossword.

"Listen to this. An American lobster fisherman cut his arm off at the elbow when he got it trapped in a winch. Imagine that. And a hiker in Utah cut his arm off when he got it lodged between a boulder and a canyon wall. Seriously, can you imagine that? That's what I call the will to survive. The eye of the tiger." Carl sang the *Rocky II* theme for a bit.

Carl banged on about some American pioneer called Peg Leg Smith, who had apparently got his name after he sawed his lower leg off with a knife in eighteen twenty something. Even the rugby fan who'd cut off his own testicles to honour a bet got Carl all fired up, and not because he thought the man was the fuckwit the media had made him out to be.

Carl was less impressed with some of the more narcissistic DIY surgeons though.

"A man who thought his skin was too loose," he read, "staple-gunned the sides of his face. Christ. And this woman cut into her thighs and tried to squeeze the fat out. Oh my God, and there's this other woman who sandpapered her face to try and get rid of her acne scars! Did you know that some people actually give blood over and over again because they think it will make their red skin appear paler?" Carl shook his head in dismay at such vanity.

On the other hand Carl admired the tenacity of the woman who'd injected local anaesthetic into her own head and then cut away a piece of her scalp and drilled into her skull till she almost died. A valiant attempt at home-trepanning to improve – or so she mistakenly believed – the way her brain functioned.

When I found the video from Carl's camcorder, it was like Chekhov's loaded gun going off in the third act of a two-hour TV detective drama. Chekhov's loaded gun. The prop device Carl himself introduced to me in the first act when he was filming himself licking batteries in the corridor. A loaded gun that – along with Carl's nonobrow and his missing teeth – I'd been too stupid to notice and take the bullets out of or replace with blanks or strawberry jelly.

Carl had taken a week off work to visit his parents in Edinburgh and I was bored. Really bored. It was a Tuesday, so Janie wasn't at work either. I couldn't pass the time gazing longingly at the back of her head while she typed or read *Cosmopolitan*. I couldn't pretend to write emails while I listened to her talking to someone on the phone.

I switched on the office TV and watched a programme about a young couple who wanted to move away from London to Cornwall to set up a bed and breakfast business or open a surf shop or maybe a small restaurant – they didn't seem to know what they wanted to do, other than get out of London. They'd already sold up and left their London flat. They said they were practically living their lives in storage and it felt like I was watching art not so much imitating my life as taking the piss out of it. I changed channels. On the other channel I caught the end of an advert for Big Yellow and figured there was a media conspiracy against me. I switched off the TV before the advert voiceover could complete the curse by saying the company's name. Speaking the name of our jaundiced nemesis out loud in this place was a bit like mentioning the name of the Scottish play in a theatre.

I decided to put a video on. There were six films to choose from in the office. The kind of videos that always used to be on the tourbus when I was in a band. Films like *Caddyshack* and *European Vacation*, anything with Chevy Chase. Both those films were in the office on a shelf underneath the TV. As were a couple of other old tourbus driver favourites: *Rambo: First Blood* and *Kindergarten Cop*.

The fifth of the six office videos was an aerobics workout video and the last tape turned out to be one of those battery operated VHS cassette adaptor things that looks like a videotape but it opens up and you can slot a smaller VHS camcorder tape into it so you can play it in a normal video machine. I'd draw a picture to illustrate what I mean but I don't think it would help. There was a camcorder tape already inside the adaptor and I stuck it in the machine.

The video began with a second or two of Carl licking a battery on that first day I'd met him. I watched him with his eyes closed as he touched the battery to his tongue, winced slightly and broke into a broad smile. Then the action on the video switched to film of Carl in the corridor wearing a plastic Groucho Marx nose, moustache and glasses get up. The camera panned down – I remembered that it was me who was doing the filming that day – to reveal Carl's plastic joke shop tits and it was like looking at the old photographs of my crazy dead dad all over again. What would Sigmund Freud have made of all this?

After the joke shop Groucho mask and tits footage things turned ugly. I think what I watched next was what they call car crash TV.

When Carl had started removing his own teeth he wasn't going to be a backstreet £1-a-tooth-wrenched-from-your-bleeding-mouth-with-a-pair-of-rusty-carpentry-pincers-after-drinking-half-a-bottle-of-cheap-scotch-dentist. Oh no. Carl had a book.

The self-surgery book that Carl had chosen from the mobile library was open on his kitchen table. Next to the book was an enlarged photocopy of what I guessed was a Polaroid picture of the inside of his mouth, and about two dozens cans of squirty cream.

I watched Carl on video as he sat down at his kitchen table and looked into the lens of his camcorder set up on his rickety tripod in front of his cooker.

"I will now begin the removal of tooth number eleven, a dog tooth. This is going to hurt, but only a little." A little bit of dentist humour for both the camera and the patient and then he took about fifty hits of Nitrous Oxide from the squirty cream and with a small make-up mirror held in front of his face, Carl started to cut into his gum with a scalpel.

The amount of blood surprised Carl and surprised me too. He must have wished he had a nurse in a white coat and tennis shoes and one of those mouth Hoovers to hook over his bottom lip and a tiny metal sink to spit the blood into. Carl screamed. I almost fainted. God knows how he didn't.

He took another ten squirts or so of Nitrous Oxide and tried to get a hold of tooth number eleven with his surgical pliers. From his face I knew it must have been like chewing silver foil while somebody scratched their fingernails down a blackboard. At first Carl's grip on pincers and tooth slipped, scraping away the enamel. The poor quality of the camcorder microphone took the edge off the horrific screech of metal on tooth but it was still unpleasant enough to make me wish I was deaf.

Through the gaps between my fingers I watched as Carl tried again. This time the stainless steel of the dental torture tools would have touched dentine: what Carl's book would have told him was the inner layer and the bulk of the tooth. He would have felt the pain right through the pulp, the very core of his tooth, where all the nerves and blood vessels are. And then the pain would continue on its journey, right on down to the thin bone-like layer – the cementum – around the root connecting what was left of Carl's tooth to his jaw. No amount of laughing gas would stop him from crying at this latest pain. Somehow he stayed conscious.

Carl battled through the pain and tried once more with the pincers until he had a firm grip on his tooth and he pulled and twisted and twisted and pulled, his tooth creaking and squeaking in his bleeding gum like a loose floorboard or the door of a haunted house. He dropped the make-up mirror and held the pliers in both hands and wiggled the tooth back and forth like a stubborn nail, until tooth number twelve, that's number twelve, a premolar, a chewing tooth, the wrong tooth, shot across the kitchen and down the back of the fridge. I wanted to shout stop, you fucking idiot, stop. And then I wanted to at least tell him where the tooth had landed.

The pain seemed to subside temporarily and the Nitrous Oxide lived up to its nickname as Carl began to laugh. And then the pain returned as Carl sat in his kitchen spitting blood into a saucepan for five minutes. Then he was back on the squirty cream with the make-up mirror, now gaffa taped to the fridge door, as he attempted to sew up the scalpel wound. Stabbing the bare bones of his jaw with the curved suture needle, causing him to collapse unconscious on his blood spattered Ikea lino. And then the office phone rang and I nearly dropped dead with a heart attack and then I had to run outside to throw up.

Stupid.

What a stupid fucking thing to do.

A few days after Carl had filmed his video nasty, and before I'd seen it, I'd brought in a game of *Operation* for us to dismantle. And Carl, who looked like Shane MacGowan and spoke with a lisp, seemed unimpressed and disinterested. I now knew it was because he had the real thing at home.

Shortly after removing his teeth and his eyebrows Carl would also shave off all his pubic hair, syringe his ears, give himself an enema and drain a pint of his own blood into a milk bottle. He also chopped off the tip of the little finger of his left hand. A casual observer would have noticed that Carl was dismantling himself. A television audience watching the violent whodunit unfold would have known. But I'd been in the dark for most of the time, accepting Carl's explanations for all his injuries and mishaps. Trapped inside the programme with Carl, waiting for my Columbo moment after the final ad break.

Even though I'd seen him since his home dentistry film, I watched the rest of the video to check Carl wasn't dead. The final image from Carl's horror kitchen was of him getting up from the floor, staggering towards the camera, all bloody-faced and toothless, to switch it off. Then the video returned to the other end of the earlier footage and a shot of Carl dressed as my dad, wobbling his joke breasts. Which was when it occurred to me that Carl might not actually be in Scotland visiting his parents.

Carl was found at home. He was on page fifty-five of his library book and a chapter entitled *Administering the Local Anaesthetic*. He was sitting on a chair next to the kitchen table where he'd removed three of his perfectly healthy teeth. The same kitchen table where he'd packed his little finger in ice until it was so cold it felt like it wasn't there at all, before slicing it off with a sharp steak knife.

Carl's book was open again on his kitchen table, next to his shiny new surgical instruments and a bottle of Xylocaine (a local anaesthetic he'd ordered from the Internet); both doctor and patient were scrubbed and gloved-up and preparing for surgery.

Just as it had done with poor old Jeffers when he'd chased the mouse into the road, curiosity would have killed Carl if I hadn't called the police and an ambulance. I pictured Carl in a surgical mask with Verdi on his stereo and a big knife in his hand and he'd be saying, "Now let's see what's under the hood."

The emergency services kicked Carl's front door in and found him in the kitchen, off his face on Internet anaesthetic and trying to find his arm with a shiny amputation saw. I don't think he could have done it. He was so doped up and if he had, I don't know if he would have survived the operation. And if he had survived, would it have stopped there? Or would Carl have then removed a foot? A leg? His appendix, his tonsils and his bollocks like that insane rugby fan?

Seven days later, under the 1983 Mental Health Act, Carl was sectioned. Look it up in the dictionary.

Adj. **sec·tioned**

1. To separate or divide into parts.

Maybe that's what he would have wanted.

PART TWO

CARL INTERRUPTED

GARY THE BUBBLEWRAP BOY

Gary the Bubblewrap Boy was a temporary replacement for Carl while he was in hospital. This isn't actually a picture of Gary but it's not far off.

DANIEL

This is the book Daniel was reading when he came to see his father at work.

This is Siegfried and Roy. Not Sigmund and Ray who put half their belongings into storage when they moved in with each other. Another coincidence.

Here's the bus I take to the hospital to visit Carl.

And this is me.

Just before this happened.

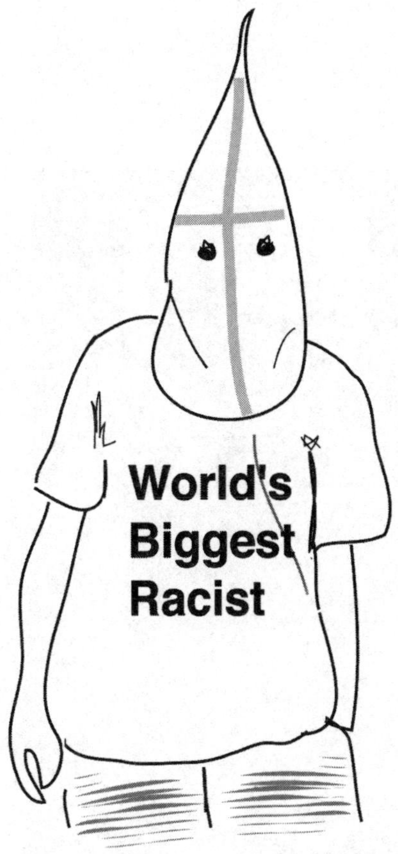

Some people say the moon landing was actually filmed in a storage warehouse. It's said that if you look closely you can see a three-piece suite, an unused home barbeque set and a depressed former rock star reflected on the glass of the visor of Buzz Aldrin's astronaut helmet.

THE STORM BEFORE THE CALM

On the night that followed Carl's sectioning, the sky was lit up by a spectacular electrical storm. I lay awake in bed and counted the seconds between thunderclaps and lightning flashes to try and calculate the storm's distance but I had no idea what the formula was for measuring it and so my conclusions were far from accurate. I was no weatherman.

I arrived at work the next morning to find seven more lowercase plastic letters (a record amount) had fallen to the ground during the storm. I picked them out of a filthy puddle one by one, like I was choosing a new set of letters in some really shitty game of giant Scrabble. An *o*, an *a*, a *g*, an *e*, a *p*, another *a* and a *c*. Twelve Scrabble points worth, presuming there were no double or treble point squares. It had been some storm. It would have made a good picture to go with that *Where Are They Now?* article in the music magazine, better than the spotty dartboard photo. A picture of me stood in a puddle beneath a foot and a half silver sign that said *arse odyssey*. If only the date on the sign would drop off.

And then Portacabin fever set in.

The power trio had imploded and I wasn't coping so well as a solo artist. I wanted the old band back together. Like it was when we were performing *Dancing Queen* and *Waterloo*. Before all the break-up songs. Before *The Winner Takes It All*.

After Carl was taken away – not by men in white coats but by men in stabvests and bright orange waterproof jackets: is nothing sacred anymore? – after Carl was taken away, and on the three days a week that Janie wasn't in, I realised it was true after all. What my headmaster had said at so many morning assemblies: the school really wasn't the building. It *was* the children.

I missed Carl. And on the days when Janie wasn't at work either, I felt like Robinson Crusoe. Those days were empty days. Not really days at all. If I could have skipped Tuesdays, Thursdays and the Saturdays that Janie wasn't in I would have. I would have voted Tory if I thought it might lead to another Three-Day Week.

On Mondays I could listen to Janie's husky timbre on the phone, talking about Sellotape and fax paper. I could pretend I was writing an important letter while I stared at the back of her impossible neck. Mondays I'd daydream of water-skiing in Paris or being badly burned on my deathbed in a derelict Italian villa. Monday I'd stalk Janie. Without ever following her home or hiding behind her hedge or stealing her rubbish or boiling her bunny. I'd stalk her from the other side of the portacabin all day, until five o'clock when she put on her coat, smiled, said goodbye and walked home to spit in her husband's dinner. I never once followed her.

It had crossed my mind.

I thought about hiding in her front garden with my guitar and serenading her with the song I'd written for her.

I'd written a song for her.

What a chump.

My Janie song wasn't a good song. I wasn't really about to sing it to her, not even from a darkened garden. Neither the song nor me were quite ready for public performance yet. My Janie song was the kind of song I'd throw cushions at if a sensitive-looking man with an acoustic guitar and a tidy beard sang it on the television.

Love songs had never been my area of expertise. All the songs I'd written in the past were about war and its futility, about man's inhumanity to man and the plight of the homeless. I'd written songs about American presidents and train strikes, about racism, homophobia and teenage gun crime. I could always manage a few verses on Palestine, Vietnam, the destruction of the planet or what it was like to sleep in a shop doorway in your own piss. But when it came to describing the curve of a neck or the colour of my true love's hair, I was no Chris de Burgh.

Perhaps one day when the song and me were ready, I'd hire a recording studio and make a CD to leave on Janie's desk or slip in her bag. Or I'd have it cut and pressed into seven-inch vinyl, with I LOVE JANIE scratched into the run out groove. I could record a B-side too. Something fast and furious about what I'd like to do to her husband. Why not a whole fucking album? Or a musical? *Janie The Musical*. Get some Arts Council backing and put it on in the West End and invite Janie along as a big surprise. Put on a suit. Win an Olivier Award, drink champagne until I felt sick and then go back to my West End hotel where I'd sleep with the show's star Juliette Binoche. Meaning Janie.

One day Janie came in to work with her arm in plaster. I wanted to write on it.

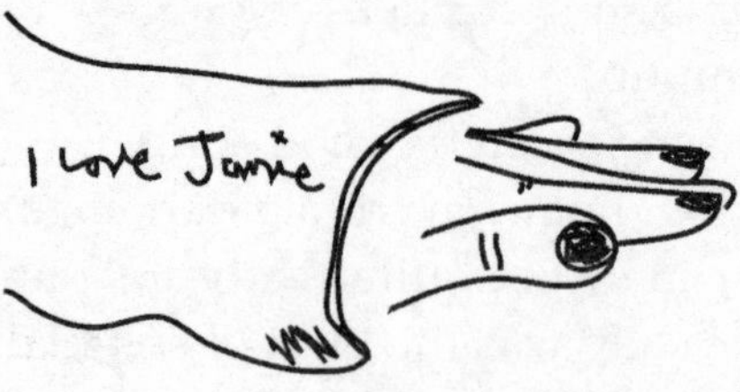

Another day she didn't come in at all. She rang to say she'd taken a nasty tumble down the stairs into a door

FLYING ANT DAY

That day that Janie lied about falling down stairs was Flying Ant Day.

The ants had turned up at least two months earlier than usual. I figured it was global warming. Everybody talks about the polar bears but no one ever mentions the ants. They're just as disorientated.

Flying Ant Day is the day that all the ants in the world check their tiny synchronised ant wristwatches and leave their nests. They swarm around, having ant sex, probably while listening to some ant music. Then the male ants drop down dead from exhaustion and the females smoke a cigarette before biting off their lover's wings and leaving in search of a new anthill or dung heap.

When I was a cruel little boy I used to empty a boiling kettle onto the unsuspecting insects as they emerged from the cracks in our garden path every summer. Not these days though. This latest Flying Ant Day I left the ants to their dirty sex games: at least somebody was having some fun. I'd save all my cruelty for the gnats. Batting and swatting them away as I walked down the nearby piss-stinking-and-rubbish-strewn-permanently-muggy-day alleyway that leads to the most miserable sweetshop in the world to buy the out of date milk and burst mint Aero that was my full English breakfast that Flying Ant morning.

It gets worse.

Can you imagine what it would be like if you woke up one morning to find out that every old wives' tale you'd ever been told was true? All the lies your mother and your aunts had told you to make you stop doing stupid things that might injure you or get you into trouble? Imagine if you woke up and discovered they weren't lies, that they weren't just clever morality tales to trick you through life without incident and arrest but that they were all cold hard facts.

Imagine that if you swallowed the pips from an apple, an apple tree *really would* grow out of the top of your head, and the same going for watermelons. Or that picking dandelions actually would make you wet the bed. That time your aunt told you that biting your tongue while you were eating was proof you were lying about something. Imagine if she meant it? And what about the time she told you that if there were twelve other people sitting at the table with you when you were eating then one of you would be dead before the year was over. Imagine what it would be like if that were true. Or if there were just three of you at the table and somebody took a photograph, then it was the one in the middle of the picture who was going to be the first to die.

You wake up one day and you're standing in front of the bathroom mirror and if you drop your comb while you're combing your hair, a year of disappointment will follow. If you're stood in front of the mirror and you pull out a grey or white hair, ten more grey hairs will grow in its place, and if it's a Friday or Sunday morning then for God's sake don't cut your fingernails, because that's bad luck, and when you do cut them, make sure you either save, burn or bury the clippings.

If your nose itches you'll be kissed by a fool quite soon. And if your itchy nose causes you to sneeze make sure you put your hand in front of your mouth or your soul will escape, with the same applying to yawning.

Your ears are burning because somebody's talking about you and if it's your left ear, that means that what they're saying about you isn't nice. Your left hand itches because you're about to lose money. If you say goodbye to someone on a bridge, you'll never, ever see them again. If you tread in a dog turd, it *really is* lucky. Have you ever woken up one morning too scared to look in the mirror because you feel like you pulled a face the night before and the wind changed while you were asleep and your face has stayed that way?

That's exactly how I felt that Flying Ant Day. Like all those old wives' tales were true.

I tried to distract myself by browsing the World Wide Web. Typing made-up names for heavy metal bands into Google and watching them all appear as actual heavy metal bands. *Six Fingered Fist* turned out to be a real band from Peru: they played *balls out, ugly fucking old skool metal. Helmut Herr* were a pierced tongue in pierced cheek death metal band from Lancashire *and Daughter Distorter's* web page motto was *Lock up your parents, here come Daughter Distorter! Satan's Bastard* were a Texan pure metal band, who boasted of their *blues-based song structures, incorporating pentatonic scales and intelligent lyrics. Kicking The Hobbit* were a no-nonsense Zeppelin-influenced rock outfit whose second album, the double concept *Tolkien No Prisoners,* was released on Japanese label *Rockin' Fist. Aaaarrrrgggghhhh!!!!,* meanwhile, were a black metal four piece based in and around Stevenage. Not to be confused with *Aaaarrgghhhh!!: dirty spunk rockers* from Falkirk with less Rs, Gs and exclamation marks than their Hertfordshire namesakes. Finally, typing *Dave Dee Dozy Beaky Mick and Bitch* into the Google images option presented me with one badly taken photograph of a six-piece poodle rock act with twin sisters (Dee and Bitch) on lead vocals.

While online I was sidetracked by various web links and pop-ups towards a lot of information that I had no idea as to whether it was true or not. *Knowledge is power,* Francis Bacon said. However erroneous, flawed or just plain wrong, Francis? 51,800 different web pages were telling me that the same Francis Bacon actually wrote all of William Shakespeare's plays and poems and even though I don't know if it's true, I'll probably tell somebody the same 'fact' one day like it is. Where's the power in that kind of knowledge? I now know but don't know that Charlie Chaplin once lost a Charlie Chaplin lookalike contest. I know but don't know that in 1989 an American toxicologist collected one hundred and thirty five different dollar bills from banks in twelve US cities and found traces of cocaine in 131 of them. I know but I have no idea if it's true that teaching children about evolution was banned by the state of Kansas because God told the state educators they should ban it. And I also don't know if there's any truth to this fact: the staff in the CIA building's snack bars are all blind in order to maintain secrecy and security. Is that really true? Can it possibly be? And did airplane manufacturers really build a special gun that fired dead chickens at their airplanes to test the strength of the windscreens? I can't be sure. Likewise I know but don't know that two Marlboro Men died of lung cancer and if I go to sleep with a mouthful of Coca Cola I'll wake up in the morning without any teeth. Or worse than that, if I fill a cat's mouth with Coke and add a packet of Space Dust or Pop Rocks, its head will explode. Missing teeth and exploding cats made me think of Carl. I wondered what he was doing now.

I used to tell jokes about the sort of things that kept me awake at night. Like, how did Dracula slick his hair back so neatly without any mirrors? Or, surely all swords are double edged?

"If owls are so wise," I'd say, "why do they keep saying Who? Who? Who?" And, "What do birds see flying around in circles when they're knocked unconscious?" Stuff like that. I must have thought I was very funny. I'd tell people I just couldn't get a good night's sleep because I wanted to know whether vultures were ever tempted to start eating themselves when they were on their deathbeds. That's the kind of hilarity I used to say kept me awake at night.

The things that kept me awake the night before Flying Ant

Day included:

1. Who was the first person to take a hose from their car exhaust and feed it back into their car as a means of suicide, and how would it have made them feel if they were to know that their pioneering method of self-death had caught on with such popularity all over the world, becoming the number one form of suicide in television dramas?

Which led me to 2. Who came up with the idea of slashing their wrists in the bath? Who wanted to end it all but didn't want to make a mess and so took their razorblades into the bathtub?

And 3. How long could I stand in the street outside this building, not doing anything? I wondered. How long would I last just standing there, minding my own business, not causing anybody any harm? How long could I stand there before I was mugged or beaten up or taken away and locked in a mental institution like Carl? I tried counting sheep, but all I could see were cows.

And I wondered whether the factory-farmed cows that gave me my pint of milk every day could still detect wet weather like they did in the old wives' tales. Did they still lie down when they sensed rain clouds forming? Did they have enough room to lie down? Those poor factory-farmed cows with their distended and overworked udders, hooked up to milking machines all day long, sucking out the milk that nature had intended for their newborn calves, newborn calves that had been snatched away from them at birth. I tried counting fluffy sheep and all I could see were these pathetic cows hooked up to machinery in tiny cubicles in vast shit-stinking cowsheds. Injected with milk-boosting hormones, impregnated again while they were still lactating, wondering where their families were. If they were lucky, their calves were in another narrow pen somewhere, sucking on an artificial teat. Unless they were milkless males and were already dead or on the back of a truck bound for Folkestone or Dover and the plate of some European veal enthusiast.

I gave up on the cows and counted sirens instead. In the hour or two that I was not falling asleep I counted fifteen different sirens: from nee naws and woo woo woos to long whining European sounding sirens that went up and down in pitch. Part of me hoped the sirens were those of ambulances or fire engines and not police cars. A house on fire – somebody else's house – or a fatal car crash. Something terrible happening to somebody else instead of me. If I couldn't smell burning and I wasn't in a car, I must be safe. I might get to sleep yet. Police sirens on the other hand meant there was a killer on the loose, heading my way, working their way through the back gardens. There were violent gangs on the run and looking for somewhere to hide before the helicopters and Alsatian dogs were mobilised. They could be outside now. Crack and smack crazed nutters, licking their lips and crowbarring my front door.

The part of me that selfishly hoped somebody else was dying in a fire, under a truck or in the back of an ambulance was the same cold hearted part of me that was always relieved when an at first apparently random murder or vicious assault on the news turned out to be committed by someone known to the victim and not so random after all. They were dead but I was safe. That's the sort of thing that kept me awake these days.

I logged off of the Internet and spent what was left of the morning trying in vain to find where that burnt lettuce smell that had lingered in the office for so long was coming from. I then wasted a good ten minutes looking at my reflection in the back of a spoon, wondering whether it made me look more like Keith Moon or Pete Townsend and whether I should grow a beard or have a shave. I reached a happy compromise by drawing moustaches on all the weirdo pictures in that month's copy *of Mini-Storage Messenger*. A further half an hour or so of my day went on practicing saying out loud some of the words I've never been able to pronounce. Words that have always twisted my tongue more than any red and yellow lorries ever did: the two worst offenders being *certificate* and *statistic*.

At twelve o'clock things picked up a bit when my new gas-lift office chair arrived. I had my swivel back. I managed to pass a good half an hour moving myself up and down with the gas lift-lever. It made a satisfying whooshing sound, like the doors opening on the deck of the Starship Enterprise. Then somebody came in to borrow a pen and after that it was nearly one o'clock and I gave myself the rest of the day off and went to see Carl.

If I timed the journey to the hospital right the bus station would be quiet. Between the hours of nine thirty in the morning and half three in the afternoon the only people waiting for a bus would be a few old age pensioners on their way to Marks and Spencers for a cappuccino and a soft biscuit. After three thirty, once the pips went and the school gates were open, the bus station belonged to the school kids and to anarchy and chaos.

After three thirty the school kids annexed the bus station. Smoking and spitting and fighting and swearing their way to the front of the bus queue. Barging through the back exit doors of the bus and up the stairs to the top deck to scratch their names into the windows and seats and scroll through the annoying new ringtones on their Nokias. I learned to time my hospital visits so that I could catch the bus with the old dears, see Carl and make it back before the school day ended.

The psychiatric hospital where they were keeping Carl wasn't the Hogarth horror engraving of Bedlam I was expecting. It was a far saner place than the bus station. The walls were decorated in the colours of a toddlers' early morning television show. All primary red and blue, green and y****w.

The hospital had its own art gallery, a place to hang all the occupational therapy paintings and drawings, including a few by well-known artists who had been patients themselves in the past. There were ping-pong tables, air hockey and baby football games and nice vinyl sofas in a communal TV and games area. It was more like a student union bar than a mental hospital.

On my visits to see Carl I didn't encounter any bug-eyed women staggering around in piss stained nightdresses with their arms outstretched, dribbling and dry humping my leg. It was nothing like *One Flew Over The Cuckoo's Nest* either. No

Nurse Ratched or Danny DeVito. No Mantovani. There was music, but it was just R and B, playing softly on a transistor radio somewhere. Most of the patients looked more bored than insane. It could have been a Tuesday afternoon back at work.

There was a hospital restaurant that served organic food: couscous, quiche, Kettle Chips and fruit smoothies. On the restaurant walls there was yet more occupationally therapeutic art. It was nice. Maybe worth going mad for. The first time I went to visit him, Carl was in the restaurant. He was picking the sultanas off a scone and arranging them in a sticky fruity stripe around the edge of his plate. I bought myself a grande mocha frappuccino and a slice of chocolate and beetroot cake and sat down with him. I took his greasy red baseball cap out of my jacket pocket and placed it on the table between us. We sat together, hardly speaking.

Carl was on a ward with all the self-harmers that he really had nothing in common with. He wasn't trying to hurt himself when he pulled out his teeth or cut the end of his finger off. If anything he was self-healing. He was more doctor than patient. I should have stood on the table in the canteen and shouted it out, *"Give him a white coat and a job you fuckers!"*

When he was first committed, the doctors had placed Carl on twenty-four hour suicide watch, which was more misdiagnosis. Carl loved life. If he'd died on his Ikea operating table it would have been an accident, a stupid one but an accident. In that first week in the hospital Carl had been probed, prodded and poked like an alien abductee by various doctors and counsellors. He was on all kinds of medication. He was sedated. He was tranquilized. He still had no eyebrows. I didn't know what to say. He had nothing to say. I felt uncomfortable; I wasn't good in these situations and couldn't stop looking at my watch and at the clock on the wall.

It was 2.42. And an hour earlier on my broken Disney watch. I'd have to leave soon to catch the bus back before the children of the damned were let out.

I was a shit hospital visitor. I hadn't brought anything for Carl. No grapes or colouring books. I had wanted to bring him a small loop the loop of Scalextric and a couple of cars but the goths and ghosts who were on the ward with him didn't look like they'd provide much motor racing competition. The table tennis and foosball tables looked particularly dusty and neglected and everyone just looked too tired. Besides, if I had brought the Scalextric in Carl might have started licking the track, which would only confuse the doctors and possibly extend his stay in hospital.

I wanted to tell Carl about what he'd missed at work and how it wasn't all that much. I wanted to tell him that if anybody was missing anything it was me. And what I missed was him. I also wanted to tell Carl how I'd gone stupid for Janie. How I'd had a Juliette Binoche film night at home. Imagining myself as her male love interest in each movie. I knew Carl would find it amusing that I'd watched the film *Chocolat* and imagined myself as the Johnny Depp character. With Juliette Binoche giving me some chocolate and me telling her how it wasn't my favourite. Carl would have laughed and told me I was lookaliking above my weight, thinking I was Johnny Depp.

I'd rehearsed an amusing anecdote in my head on the bus to the hospital about how the day after my Binoche fest Janie had asked me if I wanted anything from the most miserable sweetshop in the world. And I'd asked her to get me a Mars bar because that was my favourite. Like Depp says to Binoche in *Chocolat*. And then how I'd said to Janie that maybe a Mars bar from that particular shop wouldn't have been my favourite. Because it would be all coated with candle wax and looking like antique dog shit. But I didn't get to tell Carl my anecdote. Maybe another time.

I also didn't want to tell Carl about his temporary van driving replacement Gary the Bubblewrap Boy. I wanted Carl to believe he was indispensable and that he'd soon be better and back behind the wheel of the van himself. I wanted to believe that too.

GARY THE BUBBLEWRAP BOY

When Gary the Bubblewrap Boy was sent over from the temp agency he was wearing a big pair of sunglasses, a brown T-shirt, and jeans that were a couple of sizes too small for him. Down by his side he carried a lit cigarette. He looked like that man on the front of the Fatboy Slim album.

It was Janie who gave Gary his Bubblewrap Boy epithet.

We seemed to be getting through alarming amounts of bubblewrap since Gary's arrival. Like everybody was suddenly storing a hell of a lot of pottery and glassware. We kept running out of bubblewrap and had to give people old newspapers and magazines to wrap their crockery and mantelpiece nick-nacks in. Newspapers and magazines! It was like the dark ages.

And then Janie saw Gary in the back of the van, bursting all our bubblewrap. It turned out that from his very first day here he'd been spending his lunch breaks popping the plastic packaging bubbles until his fingers were cramped, almost contracted into claws, so he couldn't drive the van. Janie called it the Pringles effect. She said that once Gary popped he couldn't stop.

One day I heard the 4/4 beat of Sylvester's *You Make Me Feel (Mighty Real)* coming from somewhere in the building. I thought at first it was the hearing problem I'd been suffering from for about a year. Inside my head it often sounded like there was a car parked a hundred yards away with a particularly bass heavy stereo playing and the windows wide open. I could hear things that weren't there. Tube trains arriving and firework displays. I could hear my jaw moving and my eyes blinking. I heard my pulse and my footsteps and all the blood and snot and phlegm streaming through the tubes and passages at the back of my nose. I heard bongo players and somebody on the back stairs carrying a piano.

Certain frequencies of music would actually make me fall over. I'd be standing in a pub, watching a band and the singer or guitarist would hit a particular note and I'd lose my balance and topple over. People would presume I was drunk. The bouncers would throw me out.

Browsing the Internet I found out about something called Tulio's phenomenon. *Vertigo due to an opening in the bone overlying the superior semicircular canal,* it was described as. *Noise-induced vertigo, particularly around the 500Hz frequency.* The online advice was to go and see my doctor and tell him about it.

"Ah, I see," my doctor would say. "You read about it on *the Internet*. Mmmm hmmm. Now why don't you just let me do the diagnosing here? After all I am the doctor." And he'd write the words *hypochondriac* and *timewaster* down on a pad of yellow post-it notes. And that would be my appointment and the three months I had to wait for it over just like that. I'd leave the surgery with a prescription for some cotton buds and a bottle of eardrops and the same noise-induced vertigo I went in there with in the first place. On the way to the chemist I'd pass a pub, the doors would be open and a band would be sound checking. The lead guitarist would hit a note, 500Hz of sustain and feedback. And I'd fall over. So I didn't bother going to the doctor. I'd suffer in relative silence.

One afternoon I heard the 4/4 beat of Sylvester's *You Make Me Feel (Mighty Real)* and at first presumed it was just my wonky ears. I followed the disco beat towards its source at the end of the corridor, where I found a four-way extension lead plugged into another four-way extension lead that disappeared under one of the storage room doors. The one where the sound of Sylvester, accompanied now by what sounded like a basketball team practising its dribbling skills, appeared to be coming from.

I was reminded of the man who once filled a storage unit with all the footballs he'd confiscated after they'd landed in his garden. And how, when he hadn't been in for so long or paid his storage rental, Carl had to break open the padlock, and when he'd opened the door he was almost lost forever under an avalanche of confiscated footballs. That was room 98. I was past that point now, and as I got nearer to the sound of the dribbling basketballs the sound became more like the sound of earthquakes and trampolining elephants and hippopotamuses. And Sylvester's falsetto voice was still singing, *You make me feel, mi-highty-re-al.*

Every door here has a space inspired number: Apollo 1, 2, 3 etc you may recall. There's no number thirteen, not because I'm particularly superstitious, but because everybody else is. And then there's that whole ill-fated Apollo 13 moon mission. Anyway, the basketballers, the trampolining elephants and the disco music led me to Apollo 101, where the extension lead chain disappeared under the door.

Apollo 101 was the room where you might have expected to find something terrifying, like in the book *1984* or in the film if you haven't read the book. You might think I'd unlock the door of room 101 and find Richard Burton tormenting John Hurt with a cage full of rats.

Imagine the exact opposite.

I opened the door and saw Gary the Bubblewrap Boy with his eyes closed, his ghetto blaster up loud and his sound-to-light disco traffic lights pulsing between red and amber and green, red, amber and green. In time to the beat of that glorious Gay Disco tune.

Gary had hung a mirrorball from a hook in the centre of the ceiling. It was plugged into the chain of four-ways and as the mirrorball turned, it scattered specks of disco dandruff onto the pineapples and bananas on the shoulders of Gary's Hawaiian shirt. Oblivious to my presence, Gary carried on singing along to the tune coming out of his ghettoblaster. In a falsetto just like Sylvester's. Gary's tiny high voice so at odds with his huge body, turning and spinning round and around in the otherwise empty storage space.

Gary had found a way to get through his bubblewrap cold turkey. At lunchtime Gary's Room 101 was his Studio 54. There can be few happier sights left on this earth than that of a fat man dancing. I could have watched Gary all day. And that made me feel like I was cheating on Carl.

DANIEL

The last time I saw my son we argued about Carl.

"No. He isn't. He isn't a substitute son. Absolutely not. I don't need a substitute. Why would I need a substitute? You're the real thing, Dan."

"But you've never bought *me* a Scalextric track."

"I didn't buy it. We used the money from the sale of the library. We bought the Scalextric together."

"Exactly."

"What do you mean, exactly?"

"Together," Daniel said. "You bought it together. You and your substitute child." My son the smart arse.

He turned his face away. Back to his book.

I was trying to spend more time with Daniel. To make up for being one of those Hollywood cliché absent fathers: missing his kid's baseball game or school play.

I hadn't been there to comfort my son at the start of his first day at school or to welcome him home again at the end of it. I'd missed seeing him collect a book token prize from the lady mayor at the end of his first year's assembly. I didn't help him with his homework when he was younger, and now his homework was too complicated for me to understand. I was playing the optics game in a New York bar when Daniel came second in the sack race at his school sports day and I was passed out in the toilet when he won the egg and spoon.

While I'd been away on tour or doing interviews and making records and videos and acting like a child, I'd managed to miss my own child growing up.

I was kind of there when he opened his exam results.

Daniel had opened his results envelope live on breakfast television when he was just nine years old. I watched him on a TV in the foyer of the London recording studio where I was frittering away his inheritance on my latest vanity project.

"And it's a . . . grade B in computing and . . . grade A in pure maths, well done Daniel, very well done." The patronising breakfast TV presenter, with his GCSE in media studies, said.

Daniel was now thirteen and still a box of brains. Both his ships had come in at the same time. An education authority scholarship and a computer games manufacturer's sponsorship. It was enough money to spare Daniel the indignity of the local comprehensive with its national curriculum and ugly grey uniform, that would undoubtedly have been drawn on and set fire to, term after terrifying term, if teachers' pet Daniel had ever put it on.

Instead Daniel had become a boarder at a public school, where his genius would be nurtured and encouraged in a smaller classroom and on a greener sports field. A place where they'd be kind to the wunderkind and he wouldn't have to come home every evening covered in gob and chalk penises.

I didn't really know my son any better than any other boy picked at random off the street. I'd watch him now reading his fat books with the long words and big ideas, like I used to watch him sleeping in my arms, just after he was born. Cradling his delicate baby skull, that was no doubt already buzzing with knowledge, wit and insight. And I'd gently rock him back and forth and sing him to sleep, with a soft and soothing singing voice that was never captured on any of my records.

If I thought of Daniel, that was the age I'd picture him at. That's how I remember him. Not the boy genius opening the envelope on breakfast TV, or the teenager with his head stuck between the pages of a book that I'd never understand. I'm surprised he remembered me at all. Stranger danger, he must have thought whenever I knocked on his mother's door to pick him up for another uncomfortably awkward day of daddy son fun.

I knew that when Daniel gathered his books and belongings together in the camouflage backpack he kept on his back pretty much all the time, even when he was sitting down – like it was his parachute in case he had to bale out suddenly – I knew that when he put his books away and went back to his mother, there'd be no tears, only relief. There'd be no kisses goodbye between us. I might shake his hand. Sometimes I tried to high five him or ruffle his hair but he always kept his hands down at his sides or pulled his head away.

Once he was gone I hated myself for the relief I felt. I'd go and see Carl and tell him to warm up the Scalextric. I'd ruffle Carl's mullet and high five him and just stop short of kissing him. What would Sigmund Freud say about all of this?

I'd raced toy cars with Carl. I'd played hide and seek with him and soaked him with one of the giant water pistols I'd bought us both. I'd got fit with Carl, told him stories and drawn him pictures. We'd sawn golf balls in half. I'd taken him to the hospital when he was struck by lightning and sat by his bed with him till he was better. I'd done none of that with my real son. Our time together usually consisted of hanging around a grotty portacabin, Daniel reading about black holes and his father thinking of ways to get his company out of one. It was hardly Euro Disney or The Natural History Museum.

Aside from the fact that Daniel was now too big and I was too weak, if I'd picked him up off the ground and playfully thrown him into the air, what possible reason would he have to trust me to catch him again on the way back down?

DOUBLES

Sometimes you see a couple that have been together for so long that they've started to take on each other's characteristics. There's a song about them, it's called *When Two Become One*. It was a big hit for The Spice Girls.

Two such men came in to 2001 recently. Twins, identical in every single way, apart from the fact they were born on different days to two completely different sets of parents.

It was a triumph for nurture over nature and for the power of love (another song: Frankie Goes To Hollywood, Jennifer Rush, Huey Lewis and The News, among others).

It was like these two men had been separated at birth. De-conjoined twins. Joined twins. With their identikit faces and their matching facial tics, coughs, sneezes and hiccups, both of them built like the same brick shit-house. Big, tall and wide like the clothes shop that stocked everything in their size but nothing in their style. These two oversized peas in a pod, talking in the same happy monotone and laughing the same laugh. They finished each other's sentences, both of them knowing what the other was thinking and already agreeing with what they were about to say.

It's believed that everybody in the world has a double somewhere, their doppelganger. An evil twin who casts no shadow or reflection in a mirror. I've also heard of bilocation, the phenomenon that allows one person to be in two places at the same time. But here were two people in one place at the same time.

They introduced themselves like policemen with bad news.

"Good morning, my name's Ray and this is Sigmund."

Sigmund and Ray. Jesus Christ, I felt like the checkout girl at Asda when Michael Stipe hands over his Switch card. I wanted to say, "Sigmund and Ray? Were your parents big magic fans? Which one of you was attacked by the tiger? You're the world's greatest magicians. If you've got too much stuff in your house can't you just make some of it disappear?"

And Sigmund and Ray would then have to explain that, no, that's Sieg*fried* and *Roy*.

I asked them how much space they needed

"Ooh. How do you measure something like that?" They both said in unison.

If they'd gone elsewhere they could have measured it by using something called an online space calculator before they arrived. At the Big Yellow they could have typed in how many beds, chairs, tables, golf bags and lawn mowers or whatever into the space calculator on their website, clicked on the word *calculate* and watched an estimate of how much space they'd need magically appear on the screen.

But as they'd come here and our website server was down – and even if it wasn't, we didn't have an Internet space calculator – they'd just have to use their imagination. They'd have to measure the space that whatever it was they wanted to put into storage was currently occupying and guess.

"Well, we mainly want to store a few of our CDs and records, a few books and some paintings. The usual things," Ray said. "We've just realised that half the space in our flat is taken up by duplicates. Sigmund and I have almost exactly the same records and CDs as each other. We've got bookcases full of the same books, hundreds of videos and DVDs with the same films on. We've got everything twice. Things that we could only ever need one of."

I suppose if you're going to have as much in common with your partner it's good to give yourself a head start. You might find your relationship sails more smoothly if you choose somebody who already has similar tastes in music and films as you. Opposites may well attract but if they're planning on spending the rest of their lives together, they're bound to fall out at some point over whether to buy brown bread or white, or which actor was the best Doctor Who.

So Siegfried and Roy – only joking – Sigmund and Ray brought in half of their records, CDs and books and all their other doubles. Ray's *Encyclopedia Britannica* collection, Sigmund's print of Jack Vettriano's *The Singing Butler,* a scratched copy of Pink Floyd's *Dark Side Of The Moon,* the one with *Ray rools ok!* written on the sleeve. They consolidated their two Monopoly sets by removing the top hat and the Scotty dog from Ray's set and putting it into Sigmund's less tattered and more complete set. They put the Monopoly leftovers into storage.

Sigmund and Ray performed a trick that their Las Vegas near namesakes would have applauded. They put all their things into a room, locked the door and returned home to find – abracadabra – it was all still in their flat. An *Encyclopedia Britannica* collection was still in the bookcase, Jack Vettriano's *The Singing Butler* hung on the front room wall, Pink Floyd's *Dark Side Of The Moon* was still there filed under P by Sigmund, although it was no longer written on or scratched. Sigmund and Ray could still play Monopoly and there were now enough pieces for seven of their friends to play too. And on such a pristine-looking board. Magic.

Come into my tent and cross my palm with silver and I'll tell you how meanwhile, in a galaxy *far, far away*, sitting in his office being interviewed for a Sunday newspaper supplement, is an old man with long white hair and beard, wearing a baggy sweatshirt. Perhaps at first glance you'd think he was a nineteen sixties or seventies throwback, an old hippy, Jerry Garcia or Kris Kristofferson, that kind of look. He was in fact Professor Klein, Head of the Department of Gene Expression and Development in Munich. You may have read about him in another Sunday supplement under the heading *Cat Cloner*.

For upwards of $50,000 Professor Klein copied cats for rich pet lovers in the United States. People who just couldn't bear to lose their beloved Fifis and Tallulahs. Who wanted their moggies to live for more than the usual nine lives. Cloned cats for fat cats. Or *KopyKats* as it would say on the invoice.

It started with a fish.

In the sixties a Chinese embryologist took the DNA from the cell of a male carp, injected it into a female carp's egg and created the world's first cloned fish. Professor Adelfried Klein was a young science student at the time and he was inspired. One day he too would make fish. He'd also make mice and rabbits and monkeys and pigs and who knows, maybe even cats and dogs.

One day he'd clone a human.

Just seven years after the cloning of the Chinese carp and a whole quarter of a century before the more famous Dolly the sheep, in between the carp – let's call him Colin – between Colin the carp and Dolly the sheep, and thirty odd years prior to the cloned cows and various unnamed mice, rabbits, fruit flies and rats, Professor Klein cloned his first boy.

He named him Adelfried after himself. Just as God might have done. And Klein continued playing God, cloning and alphabetically naming nineteen boys. The science world said it couldn't be done, not males, they cannot be cloned. Females yes, but males no.

But that's what Professor Klein did. Nineteen boys. Adelfried, Brandeis, Cort, Dieter and Ernest. All the way through the alphabet to Omar, Peter and Quentin, with each new boy eventually dying but living just that little bit longer than the last. It was this that kept the professor going, putting himself through the pain of the grieving parent time after time. He hoped he would one day rid himself from that worst of all things for a parent. Outliving your own children.

The professor's work was conducted illegally and in secret. In back rooms of deserted private hospitals and deep in the basements of empty office blocks. All across Europe and in Shanghai and Beijing, just him and his assistant with the bad posture, brought on by spending his teenage years locked up in his bedroom reading science books and looking at slides under his microscope. Klein's assistant didn't have a stoved in face or Marty Feldman bug eyes and he wasn't called Igor but he was at least entering into the spirit of things by being a bit of a hunchback.

Professor Klein's cloned boys, from Adelfried to Ernest, lived for a very short while and then died, breaking Professor Klein's heart and strengthening his resolve. He carried on his work: through Frederick, Geert and Horst who lived to be old enough to eat solid food, and Imre, who could ride a bicycle without stabilizers before he died. Then there was Kellen, Leo and Manfred, each miraculous boy living slightly longer than the last. There were thirteen candles on Nikolas' cake a week before his underdeveloped lungs ceased to function and his younger brother Omar survived for fourteen and a half years until his enlarged heart stopped beating. Quinten looked as though he might live forever only to be brutally bludgeoned to death by a junkie who'd broken into one of the professor's makeshift labs looking for drugs.

Heartbreaking.

And then there were the surrogate mothers. For every limelight-hogging superstar like Dolly the sheep there was an anonymous ewe surrogate behind the scenes. Whether for money or because they had children of their own and couldn't imagine how terrible it would be to not be able to have children of their own and just wanted to help.

For the surrogate mothers these were especially uncomfortable pregnancies. All the cloned boys were twice, sometimes three times the size of naturally born boys. To some people they would have been thought of as freaks and so although Klein wanted to show off his boys he only took them out into the world when they needed to move from one deserted hospital or office block basement to another.

In an empty hotel building where the Professor had set up his final laboratory and temporary home for the only two surviving boys, Professor Klein's assistant found an old Bible. Left behind for him in a drawer by those omnipresent hotel guests The Gideons. The professor's assistant started to read the Holy book and began to see that what he and the professor were doing was wrong. One night he put the boys into the back of a cab and disappeared.

The professor spent weeks looking for his sons. He searched every empty room of the empty hotel. In the en-suite bathrooms and wardrobes and then out into the streets he searched. He looked for them right across the city and deep into the surrounding countryside. He placed small ads in the same newspapers he'd used to advertise for surrogate mothers but found nothing. He hardly slept or ate, grieving more for his two living lost boys than he'd done for any of his dead children. It was the not knowing that upset him so, the hope that hurt so much. After Raimund and Sigmund, Professor Klein stopped cloning boys. He couldn't make it to the end of his alphabet. He just didn't have the heart for it anymore. Eventually, a lonely and broken man, he packed up and went home to clone cats.

Seated at his desk in his baggy sweatshirt, with his crazy white hair and his Jerry Garcia beard, he was telling it all to the Sunday papers.

"It is impossible to create two identical human beings. They are not identical at all. They may as well be chalk and cheese. Their fingerprints would be different. No, no. Only the clone's chromosomal or nuclear DNA will be the same as the donor's." And the professor talked to the Sunday magazine about nurture versus nature. "Most twins are born, others are created over a sustained period of living together. Nurture will, I believe, always win in the long run. It is entirely possible for identical twins, for example, to be separated from each other and become completely different, identical in looks only.

"By the same token, two completely unrelated individuals could become as completely identical as twins by spending prolonged periods of time together." And he'd been talking for too long now, he was tired and had to keep clearing his throat, his voice cracking like he was about to cry.

Dolly

On my second trip to the psychiatric hospital, Carl was more upbeat. He even talked about his attempted self-op.

"I won't be trying anything like that again."

I think he also said he was going to put himself together again but I might have just wished that he'd said that. Carl told me his mum and dad had been to see him.

"They drove down from Scotland overnight. With *stuff*."

Carl reached down beneath the hospital restaurant table to pick up a supermarket carrier bag from which he started producing things his parents had brought to the hospital for him. He pulled them from the bag like rabbits from a magician's top hat.

"A banana!" Carl announced. "An orange! Another orange. An apple. A magazine. Some Edinburgh rock, like they've just come back from holiday from the city they live in, and..." Carl took a brown envelope from the magic carrier bag, A4 sized folded down to A5. "Cash!" he said, handing the envelope across the table to me. "It's money from my dad. I don't know what he thinks I'm going to do with it in here, or anywhere else really. It's all in Scottish five-pound notes. Would you keep it safe for me till I get out?"

I took the envelope and put it on the seat under my leg.

I curved my hand to make a C sign to ask if Carl wanted a refill for his coffee and he replied with one hand placed on top of the other in the international sign for tea.

"Builder's? Two sugars?" I asked and he gave me a Cub Scouts in the local newspaper double thumbs up.

I went up to the counter of the hospital restaurant and ordered Carl's tea and a tall black Americano for myself – which made the woman behind the counter laugh. I brought the drinks back to the table, sat down and told Carl how there'd been a fight at work.

"Hey, Carl. I went in extra early this morning, to sort a few things out, and I found Pinocchio with a panda in a headlock; he had his arm around the panda's neck and he was beating it repeatedly about the face with the wooden crutch of a young boy who'd been stamping his callipered foot into Oliver Hardy's face nearby. Stan Laurel was swinging from the disabled boy's shoulders, pulling his hair."

I was talking without pause for breath, like I was commentating on a horse race. I knew this story well. I'd practiced it in my head on the way to the hospital.

"And meanwhile Bruce Lee and Mister T were beating all kinds of crap out of a sweet-looking little girl and her teddy bear. They were showing off their martial arts chops and street fighting moves. It was a total bloodbath. A blind boy had his stool kicked from under him and his little yellow pullover was pulled over his head by Lara Croft and the blind kid was scrambling about on the floor with his teeth sunk into the ankles of a livid Boy George. There was loose change and wood splinters all over the floor. Oh yes, of course, *now* I know that I shouldn't have put that collection of old four-foot high charity collection boxes in the room next to Geppetto's pine people. Of course I realise that *now*."

Carl laughed a sit-com laugh, spitting cake crumbs and snorting his tea all over the table, causing some of the hospital staff to look up from their lunches. A short Asian woman in a white coat who looked like that actress who was in *Bend It Like Beckham* and went on to star in *ER*, seemed to be taking notes. They thought Carl was madder today than he was yesterday. I knew he was getting better. Next time I came to see him I'd print him a copy of HAL's murder confession. I might even tell him about Gary the Bubblewrap Boy disco dancing in his Hawaiian fruit shirt. Carl would be cured within no time. They'd make a Hollywood movie about my revolutionary psychiatric treatment. Robin Williams would get the Oscar for playing me. In his acceptance speech Williams would thank God, his agent, the director and the producers but most of all me. The constant audience applause in the Kodak Theatre would threaten to go on forever until I reluctantly stood up and made a little humble bow. After the awards ceremony I'd go to Elton John's Oscar party and drink champagne until I felt sick, when I'd go back to my Hollywood hotel for Titchmarsh sex with Juliette Binoche. Meaning Janie.

One day Janie would be a wrinkly old lady.

I'd still love her though. I knew all that smiling would have to leave creases but I expect I'd prune with age myself. Although with me it would be more frown furrows than laugh lines. There was always Botox.

If she was with me, Janie would never feel the need to sneak out of bed to watch late night TV education programmes ever again. We could buy a sweetshop together. A happy sweetshop. The most happiest sweetshop in the world. We'd be Mr and Mrs Willy Wonka. Handing out golden tickets. And when Carl got out of hospital he could be our Oompa Loompa.

And then it happened.

Janie came in to work and said three words.

Three wonderful little words.

And everything changed.

“NICK

IS

DEAD."

The day hadn't started out quite so wonderfully. It was a Saturday and not one of Janie's Saturdays. So I was fed up. Bored. If I'd been keeping a diary it would have read something like:

> Saturday
> *Morning – Tapped my fingers on the desk till elevenses: half a cup of weak coffee (not enough granules in the jar for a full cup); the milk is turning. Go to miserable sweetshop for a fresh pint and small emergency jar of coffee. Man behind counter makes me guess the price of my milk and cheapo coffee powder. Expect to use whole jar to make a cup of coffee that's actually strong enough to drink. Can't find spoon and have to stir coffee with pen and get tiny drop of blue ink on surface of coffee; lift inkblot off with finger and wipe on jeans.*
>
> *After elevenses, check company finances. May not be enough cash flow to pay staff. Owners say to let Janie go, employ part time university student instead. If Janie goes then I go, is what I want to say.*
>
> *Midday – Tried to untie a knot in the lace of my shoe for almost thirty minutes. Give up and cut through lace. Walk around with a limp for the rest of the day trying to keep shoe from falling off. Eventually use piece of garden string as temporary shoelace. It'll still be there in a month's time. Another fifteen minutes wasted on trying to read what it is I wrote on the back of my hand last night.*
>
> *Lunchtime – Eat half of the most disappointing sandwich of my entire life. Remove most of the salad, as it tastes bad. Think I actually broke a tooth on a piece of lettuce. After shit lunch try and remember all the women and girls I've been*

intimate with in my life. Alphabetise them. Sixteen letters short of a full alphabet. Reaching the letter R, I remember my sister Robin and how I haven't seen or spoken to her for such a long time. I keep promising to visit her in Sydney but my passport has expired. Must get new passport photos done. Every time I do I always seem to look like Carlos the Jackal. They'd never let me on the plane. To be honest I'm scared of flying. All those different flights around the world when I was in a band must have upped the chance of me being in a plane crash. Surely.

Thinking about Robin makes me think about my dad and then my mum and it's like family guilt dominos. The final domino to topple is my son Daniel and the last time I saw him when we argued about how I was spending more quality time with Carl.

Just as I thought I couldn't feel any more like a nobody, a man came in and mistook me for a somebody.

I thought he was one of those serial killers. Looking for a private place to offload his freezer full of gore. Then I thought he probably needed some space to house the vast collection of illegal pornography that was piling up in his fetid masturbatorium of a bedsit. Or somewhere quiet to build his pipe bomb. When he walked in through the door of the portacabin he did an immediate double take and practically shouted at me.

"What the hell are you doing here? Did you fake your own death or something?"

And I had to have that conversation again. The whole bit. His disbelief that I could actually be in need of money enough to have to do a proper job. I had to pose with him for the camera phone picture that was too dark the six times he attempted to take it, holding his phone at arms length in front of us like a sparkler. Then there was the screwed up bus ticket I had to sign my name on and that he hilariously said he was going to put on ebay.

"Don't you miss it though? I bet you do," the porn-collecting pipebomber said after I signed another autograph, this time for his friend Martin. "I bet you miss the fame."

And I sighed. Exhaling from right down in the very depth of my very being, so the whole world moved an inch or two to the left and Canada sank into the Atlantic.

Because of course sometimes I did miss the fame. Who wouldn't? I was always jealous when a band came in here, buzzing with excitement at the start of a tour to collect their guitars and amps. Or when they returned at the end of the tour, tired and hungover, to put whatever they hadn't lost back. The Pornobomber was right; the customer always is. Sometimes I really missed the fame.

"You must be loaded."

And again the stupid fucking customer was right. I was loaded. So very loaded. Cocked and locked. Full-metal-jacket. That's exactly the reason why I was sat in that crappy hut of an office, typing his details into what must be one of the world's first ever computers that had just crashed again. I was loaded. I was the richest man in Britain. I had more money than Elton John knew what to do with. This was just my hobby. It was the loneliness and the mind-crushing tedium that I particularly enjoyed. I'd been chased down Tokyo streets by teenage girls; I'd been the centre of attention; I'd experienced what it was like to be vastly overpaid for something I actually enjoyed doing. I used to make a long list of whatever alcoholic drinks and drugs that I fancied abusing my body with for the day. I'd give the list to somebody and they'd go to the off licence and the local pusher and get it all for me. They'd put all the booze and drugs and more fruit than Covent Garden Market on a table in a room with my name above a star on the door. There'd be wall-to-wall mirrors in the room, surrounded by light bulbs so I could look at myself and think that I was special.

If I was chased down the street by teenage girls now it was because they wanted to take my wallet and bitch slap and humiliate me. They wanted to see me in a newspaper story that said *KILLED! And all for £1.47 and a stale Twix!*

Before I'd left for work that morning I'd had to raid the Nescafe jar I'd been filling with the small coins that people dropped from their pockets and from down the backs of the old sofas and armchairs brought in here every week. I had to empty the coffee jar to buy what would turn out to be the most disappointing sandwich of my entire life from the most miserable sweetshop in the world – bought from the only man on the planet with less job satisfaction than me. I thought I might buy my own island.

"No, I don't miss it at all," I said, and I gave the pervert his padlock and showed him which room he should build his bomb in. The walk along the strip lit corridor, with its locked silver rooms on either side, made me think not of futuristic space adventure, but of death row. I wanted to shout "Dead man walking here!" and drag a truncheon along the corrugated doors.

"Have you ever wondered what happened to all the boybands?" I asked the Pornobomber. And as I started to explain about the football stadiums and the flightcases it made me feel just that little bit better.

Then Janie came in and dropped the bombshell about her husband.

NICK

All the time I'd been casting myself opposite Janie in various French language masterpieces and Hollywood Oscar winners, her husband was starring in his own movies. Typecasting himself again and again in the role of the abusive husband bullying his beautiful wife. He'd knocked her around in *Sleeping With The Enemy* and terrorised her in *This Boy's Life* and in what was to be his final role, he was Marlon Brando in *A Streetcar Named Desire*.

Nick Maplin's last hurrah was filmed on lo-res, poorly lit council and police CCTV cameras. It was pieced together by bored coppers and posted on an Internet video sharing website.

The action began outside the 1980s theme pub The Tony Hadley, a pub that Maplin had just been barred from. The grainy cameras outside The Tony Hadley recorded and pinpointed in place and time the start of Nick's drunken journey home.

It was 23:30:06 when he was first captured on video in the pub car park. Dressed in his wife beater vest, shouting out Janie's name like Brando in *A Streetcar Named Desire*, but instead of "Stella, Stella, Stella!" he shouted "Janie! Janie! Janie! You fucking bitch!" And then he shook his fists at the camera as though he knew he was being filmed and he made a noise like a dinosaur,

"Nnnneeeaaarrrgghhhhhggghh! Or something like that." The police lip-reader said at the inquest.

Nick had been out for the night with his wife and his friends. It must have been a good night. He'd managed to lose his wife, his shirt, his right shoe and his car. He was so far over the legal drink-driving limit that had he found his car, driven it and been stopped and breathalysed by the police, they would have presumed there was something wrong with their breathalyser machine.

"I drive better when I'm drunk," he must have told so many people so many times.

As 23:36:53 ticked over on the counter at the bottom of the CCTV film, Nick gave up looking for his car, his wife, his shirt and his shoe and he limped out of the pub car park, pushing the closed hot dog hut over as he left.

"Come on! Let's have yer, you cunt!" He shouted at the passing traffic, the female police lip-reader was somewhat embarrassed to translate.

Nick Maplin's journey home would take him past banks and chip shops, building societies and dry cleaners, through housing estates, shopping precincts and industrial estates. All the way he followed the trail left by his junior graffiti squad.

Over railway bridges and under bus shelters his way was marked out in spray-paint. In Fiat tangerine and Peugeot brown in the doorway of the off license where he stopped to empty his bladder at 23:41:05. And a minute later in gold and silver paint on a monument to the dead of two world wars outside what used to be the library.

At precisely 23:45:00 Nick was filmed as he stopped to answer his mobile phone, noticing something fresh to graffiti as he looked at the newly opened branch of The Carphone Warehouse he was stood outside of. He made a mental note of it.

Up until fairly recently The Carphone Warehouse had been a Tandy store, selling electronic hobby kits, remote control cars and cheap electrical accessories, and then The Carphone Warehouse bought out Tandy. Nick stopped outside the new shop to answer his phone, which was vibrating and playing the melody from *Live Forever* by Oasis in the pocket of his jeans. It was a junk text message offering him a great deal on life insurance.

"I don't need your fucking life insurance fuck," he slurred into the phone, according to the red-faced police lip-reader.

At 23:45:17, as Nick Maplin stood outside the shop that used to be Tandy, as the song *Live Forever* told him to answer his phone and as he stopped to delete the mobile spam telling him his life needed insuring, a van delivering cans of spray-paint turned the wrong way down a one way street, having not seen the NO ENTRY sign that had been painted over by Nick's graffiti task force earlier that night. And as the van swerved to avoid a coach that was on its way home from a Pet Shop Boys fan club convention, it crashed through the former Tandy shop window and killed Nick Maplin.

Now *that,* Alanis Morissette, is ironic.

DESTINATION – IRONY
PSB1

One hundred thousand people attended Martin Luther King's funeral, the same number for Rudolph Valentino's, and about a million mourners showed up for Princess Diana's with another two and a half billion watching on TV. There were eleven people at the crematorium on the day that Nick Maplin was carried in in a cheap wooden box. And that was including the vicar, the undertakers and a man who goes to the funerals of people he didn't know. The majority of us were there for the widow and I think she was only there herself to make sure her husband was definitely dead. If she could have held a mirror in front of his mouth, stuck pins under his fingernails or placed a hot match on his cheek to check, I'm sure she would have.

"Did you know," I said to Janie as we walked slowly into the crematorium chapel, "it's bad luck to count the cars in a funeral cortege?"

There were four cars at Nick's funeral, hardly a cortege, not even much of a convoy. Just random people arriving. Some were late, others early, some came by bus and others walked. Gary brought Janie and me in the company van, with my son Daniel sitting on the wheel arch in the back.

"And nothing new should be worn to a funeral, especially new shoes," I said.

My suit wasn't new. It glistened and smelled from the last-minute- too-hot ironing I'd given it before we left arse odyssey. The trousers itched the inside of my thighs and there was a dried carnation in the pocket from a wedding I didn't remember going to.

Daniel didn't have a suit. He'd come straight from school the night before and wasn't planning on going to a funeral. I hadn't told his mother about it when she dropped him off. I didn't want to spoil the start of the dirty weekend she was flying to Paris with her new boyfriend Julian for by having an argument about my latest poor choice of father-son activity.

Nevertheless, Daniel was probably the smartest mourner – and I use the term mourner incredibly loosely – at Nick Maplin's funeral. Dressed in his school shirt and tie and his posh blazer: backpack and parachute still on his back, just in case the vicar lost control of the plane.

Instead of spreading ourselves about the crematorium chapel we all sat in the front row to make it clear just how unpopular the deceased was. I sat on the pew next to Janie like the father of the bride.

Janie had her head bowed.

She was checking for text messages on her mobile.

To Janie's left, Gary had his hand in his jacket pocket and above the gentle sound of recorded church organ and tape hiss I could hear popping plastic. Gary was wearing an Acapulco shirt with pictures of palm trees on it. I was winding my watch. I had the beginnings of an erection. Daniel was doing mental arithmetic. Nobody has any respect for the dead these days.

One last old wives' tale I remember was that you should never speak ill of the dead, or one day they'll come back to haunt you.

Nobody spoke ill of Nick Maplin but neither could anybody find anything that nice to stand up in a crematorium chapel and say about him, and in the end it fell to the local vicar who'd never met Nick. The vicar kept his eulogy brief and full of generic funereal cliché and misplaced praise for the dead man: calling him Dick three times and Mick twice. When the cheap coffin went behind the curtains and on to hell to the sound of Robbie Williams' *Angels* (Nick's least favourite song of all time, chosen by Janie) a cheer wouldn't have been out of place.

After the funeral we went to a wake in the same nineteen eighties theme pub where Nick had had his last ever drink and I drank champagne until I felt sick, before having filthy, far-fetched and unbelievable Alan Titchmarsh sex with Juliette Binoche. Meaning Janie.

No, really.

If the softly spoken poet Tom Paulin who used to review books, films, art and theatre on Friday's *Newsnight* programme on BBC2 had to review the love scene between Janie and me he'd say it was ridiculous and totally unbelievable. I have this vision of him now, sat in the BBC studio next to Germaine Greer.

"This is *absolutely ridiculous*. Completely unbelievable," Tom is saying in his softly spoken Northern Irish italics. Tom is saying it's possibly the most ludicrous love-making scene he's ever had the misfortune to sit through. This is what he looks like when he's making his point.

In my vision, Paul Morley and Tony Parsons are there sticking up for me.

"Oh come on Tom. That's how real people do it," Parsons says. "Quick and messy, with a broom wedged under the handle of a pub toilet door." And Paul Morley agrees, while Tom just shakes his head in despair.

At The Tony Hadley, Daniel sat in the corner reading a book and drinking a Coke, while I tried to chat the barmaid up by hinting that I might be famous. She politely wondered whether if I had to explain that I was famous, that maybe I wasn't really technically famous.

While I was thinking about this, the grieving widow Janie was drowning her sorrows in tears of laughter, her wide smile looking as though it might actually cause her head to flip open like a Janie Pez. Someone put *Agadoo* on the jukebox and Gary the Bubblewrap Boy was doing the actions: pushing the pineapple and shaking the tree. I hadn't been this happy since the days before Carl was taken from us.

Janie ordered a bottle of champagne and Gary opened it. Disappointingly – particularly for him – there was no pop. We all sat around a too-small table and proposed toasts to absent friends. Janie talked for a while about her dead husband. She told us about the one time she'd actually enjoyed his constant drunkenness. It was the night of their second wedding anniversary and her 26th birthday – Nick forgot both – and he came home tired and emotional from another long hard day at the pub. After swearing and breaking a few of Janie's favourite things, he fell over and puked himself unconscious. Janie took off her slippers, put on her wedding day high heels and kicked her comatose husband. Once for each year of their wedded bliss together, and another for each of her missed birthdays. A combined anniversary and birthday gift to herself, she said. When Janie finished talking, the table fell quiet until she lifted her champagne glass and said, "Good riddance to bad rubbish!"

And we all chinked glasses and said "To bad rubbish!" in loud voices so the barman thought we were talking about the quality of the champagne and tutted, then dropped a glass. We cheered when it smashed and the barman tutted some more.

Gary and Daniel went over to the pub trivia machine. Between the two of them they knew everything. The barman tutted with every pound coin they won.

Back at the table I got drunk with Janie.

"Have you heard of a book called *The Goth Cop*?" I asked her.

"I don't think so. What's it about?"

"It's this Welsh policeman's memoirs. There's a bit in the book about how everybody looks like somebody famous. Who do you think I look like?"

"I don't know, who?"

"No, you tell me. Is there somebody famous I look like?"

"I'm not very good at these things."

"Have a go."

Janie looked at me. For longer than she needed. Maybe that was the moment. The spark of chemistry when our eyes met properly for the first time. It's not all big bangs with chemistry. For every butane ignited and explosive fire there's got to be a bit of rust. Some slow-burning chemical reactions just waiting for a catalyst.

"I suppose in a way you look most like you."

"What do you mean?"

"You're already a famous person. You look like yourself."

"I'm hardly famous anymore," I said with genuine modesty. Janie put a reassuring hand on my leg and I felt the blood rushing to my face in a warm blush. She left her hand there and the blood left my face and began its rapid descent back down my body, past Janie's hand, and from that point, neither me, Tom Paulin nor any of the *Newsnight Review* team were in control of the situation anymore.

"Do you know who you look like?" I said, my voice shaking slightly.

"Me? No. Who?"

"Juliette Binoche."
"What, the actress?"
"The most beautiful woman in the world."

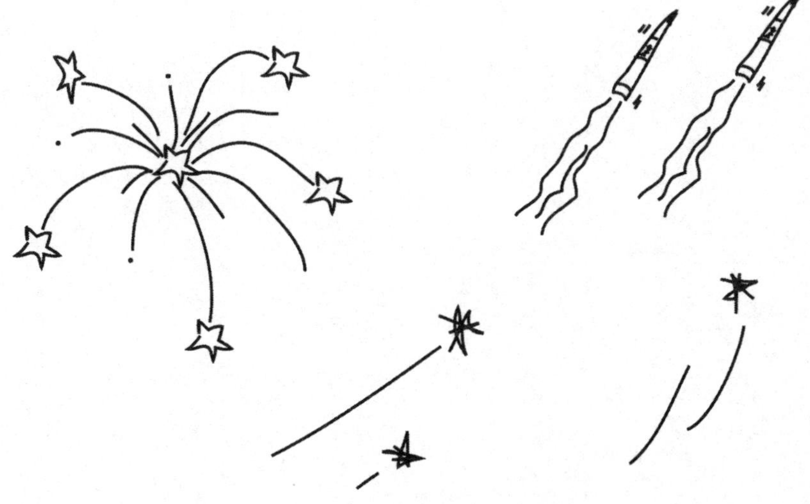

In years to come Janie's first child would ask his or her mother, much like I'd done with my own tragic parents when they told me about that hot day in London Zoo,

"Mummy when was your first date with Daddy?"

And Janie would have to lie because she didn't feel she could give the honest answer, which was:

"Well darling. It's a funny story but me and your father had our first proper date in the pub toilet at the wake that followed the funeral of my dead husband."

Nothing that took place between Janie and me in the women's toilets at The Tony Hadley was worth more than a paragraph of Titchmarsh's romantic fiction. Hardly even enough for a single verse of a Chris de Burgh song. Tom Paulin really would have hated it.

He would have hated the way it seemed to just suddenly happen. From one minute sitting talking innocently about lookalikes, to sudden frenzied kissing and fumbling in the toilet. But that's the way it happened. Like there was a jump in time, and there we were, pulling at each others funeral clothing, Janie handicapped by having her arm wrapped in Plaster of Paris and me trying to block thoughts of Paris out of my mind. My wife Karen would be in Paris. Possibly doing a similar thing with her new boyfriend Julian in a French toilet. In a French unisex toilet, better equipped for love making than the women's toilet in The Tony Hadley was. There was no Johnny machine for a start. We should have gone in the gents. But who wants to make love while standing in a puddle of urine, looking at a drawing of an ejaculating penis or at CHELSEA ARE SHIT written on the wall in a disturbing shade of brown?

Obviously having sex with a widow in a pub toilet while your thirteen year old son plays pub games in the bar with a bubblewrap fetishist might not seem like the actions of a responsible father. But when all was said and done I couldn't stop myself. Irresponsibility was my middle name. Yesterday it had been Misery but today it was Irresponsibility. Even though I'd been dropped by my record label, grown new fingerprints over my guitar-string calluses and sold my gold discs at a boot sale at a time when they weren't worth much more than the frames they were mounted in, deep down I was still a rock star. Rock stars have sex in toilets.

We wedged a broom under the door handle – it may have been a mop – and we made the best of it. Going at it like flying ants for less than five minutes, when there was a rattle of the door handle, raised voices and a familiar tut tut and shortly after we were thrown out of the same pub Janie's dead husband had been barred from less than a week ago. It was turning into quite an evening.

As we left The Tony Hadley, Daniel wanted to know why we had to do so in such a hurry. He said that he and Gary were two questions away from the trivia jackpot. I told him it was all just a silly misunderstanding, although I hoped it wasn't.

The sun had gone when we left the pub, but there was no moon. It was either late afternoon or early evening as we walked back to where Gary had parked the van. I didn't hold hands with Janie. We didn't skip. I didn't wrap my arm around her shoulders and peck at her cheek and ears.

Janie was avoiding me, power walking ahead of me, talking to Gary. Because of shame or guilt or regret or horror or disgust or dread or because I'd laddered her brand new tights and made her break a fingernail, Janie was avoiding me.

She was probably telling Gary that our romance had been just one of those things and telling him about the spur and the heat of the moment and how she should probably tell me that it would maybe be best if we forget it had ever happened and just go back to normal. Put it all down to experience. I didn't want to go back to normal. It was shit there. Fuck experience.

From talking about *The Goth Cop* at the tiny pub table, to our five-minute fumble in the toilets and to this embarrassed break up, this had been the whirlwind romance to end all whirlwind romances. Blink and you missed it. We hadn't had a chance to lie back and look up at the cobwebs on the bedroom ceiling while we shared a cigarette. I never got to say, "I thought you'd never guess. My favourite." Like I was Johhny Depp at the end of *Chocolat*.

Perhaps I'd dreamt it all. Tom Paulin would kick the *Newsnight Review* table over and hunt me down and kill me if it had all just been a dream.

As soon as Janie was alone she'd be phoning her friends to tell them how she'd made a big mistake and how she hated herself and me even more. I'd taken advantage of her when she was vulnerable and confused. When she was technically grieving for God's sake. Janie had no way of knowing how I really felt about her and for how long I'd felt that way. She hadn't heard the song I'd written about her or been at the movie festivals I'd held in my front room in her name and likeness. She just thought I'd used her for sympathy sex, just another sleazebag drunk man treating her badly. Her husband's ashes were still smouldering and already she'd found herself a new moron who couldn't hold his drink or keep his penis in his pants.

When we got to the van Gary offered to drive us all home and Janie said she didn't feel like going home yet and suggested we go back to work for a nightcap.

"One for the road," she said. "There's that box of bankrupt off licence alcopops in the office. Do you mind? I could just do with one more drink before I go home. Is that okay?"

Janie climbed in the front of the van beside Gary, and I sat in the back with Daniel, and I watched Janie's neck, trying to work out if the curve had changed.

She turned round in her seat and looked back at Daniel, "There's also a box of Coca Cola, promoting the World Cup or something." Janie looked at me too and she smiled and then we drove over a pothole and I slid off the cold metal of the wheel arch and everybody cheered.

Maybe the whirlwind romance wasn't quite blown over after all. Maybe there were still cars to be lifted up into the air and roofs to be torn off the tops of houses before it died down. Perhaps it wouldn't die down at all. God bless Mother Nature and her turbulent and unpredictable weather.

We drove back to work, not in silence and not singing *we're all going on a summer holiday* but somewhere in between. It was a bumpy ride and a couple of times I thought I might throw up because of the speed humps, the smell of petrol fumes in the back of the van and the flat champagne slushing around in my belly. I felt seasick. I stopped myself from vomiting by joining in with the wahays and the wooahs every time we went over a particularly steep bump and by talking to Daniel in between the bumps about school and what music he was into. He said he actually quite liked some of mine. I almost cried.

Back at arse odyssey Gary parked the van and we went into the portacabin for out of date fruit cocktails. Brightly coloured sickly-sweet tasting drinks with Russian looking labels: all back to front Rs and pictures of serious-faced and furry-hatted men. The retro cola Daniel and Gary drank was also out of date. A dozen cans advertising the 2006 World Cup, each one with a picture of a different French footballer printed on. Daniel had Fabian Barthez while Gary opened a can of Nicolas Anelka Coca Cola and he laughed.

"Nicolas Anelka Coca Cola, ha, ha. I like the sound of that.

Nicolas. Anelka. Coca. Cola."

"Shall we do the tour?" I asked Daniel.

"I have been here before you know," he said.

"Ah but not the full tour, though. The boybands and the shoes and the gravestones. Come on. I'll show you what the tourists don't get to see." We left Janie and Gary to talk about French footballers' haircuts and went to look at an enormous amount of shoes.

IMELDA'S SHOE MUSEUM

I showed Daniel a room full of sandals, mules and stilettos, high-heeled shoes and flats. Piled high in shoeboxes and hung from the ceiling in canvas shoe wardrobes and on freestanding shoe racks. There were lace-ups and flip-flops, Spice Girls platform shoes, tap and ballet shoes. Imelda had collected shoes made by famous cobblers like Ferragamo, Givenchy, Chanel and Christian Dior and some from the medical profession/footwear crossover: like her Dr. Martens boots and her Dr. Scholl's wooden slip-ons that Imelda had bought after Sarah Jessica Parker wore a pair in *Sex In The City*.

They say people with a lot of shoes are frustrated travellers and in spite of the fact that Imleda had bumper boots from India, monkey boots from Czechoslovakia, Cuban heels, Spanish espadrilles, Italian loafers and Swiss moon-boots, she had clearly never been anywhere.

I showed Daniel a pair of posh patent leather evening shoes behind glass on a display rack of their own, and I showed him scuffed Dunlop plimsolls thick with re-whitener. I showed him a pair of hippy shoes that looked like Cornish pasties. I showed him winkle pickers, beetle crushers, brothel creepers, two pairs of waffle stompers, one bowling shoe and no trainers.

"The one time Imelda came in here," I said to Daniel, "she

took off the shoes she was wearing at the time and I swear she walked with high-heeled feet."

We nicknamed Imelda after the former Philippine First Lady and shoe fetishist Imelda Marcos. A woman who once quipped that when she fled the Philippines with her husband, "They went into my closets looking for skeletons, but all they found were shoes, beautiful shoes."

"Which is kind of spooky," I said to Daniel as I shut the door on Imelda's shoes, leaving the smell of leather and cheese in the air. "Because when our Imelda had gone into her closet at home to clear out all her shoes to bring them in here," I continued, locking the door, "she found a skeleton. Onwards." And I started walking deeper into the warehouse.

"Hang on. What skeleton?" Daniel said, following me down the corridor.

"If you really want to know, you'll have to wait until the end of this tour. Or…" I stopped in my tracks, dramatically. "If you're just too impatient and you really need to know right now, well, I *can* tell you now. But as you'll soon realise once I start telling you, there may be unfortunate consequences for such impatience. The choice is yours."

"I'll wait," Daniel said.

"Very well, child," I said, in a comic Transylvanian or thereabouts accent. If I was wearing a cape I would have swept it around myself like a bat's wings and cackled as I began walking again along the corridor.

"Isn't this trespassing?" Daniel asked as I unlocked the second door to reveal a roomful of flat batteries belonging to someone we called Battery Man.

"Technically, maybe it is," I opened the door anyway. "All these batteries would be a thrill for Carl if they weren't all flat."

"Why's that?" Daniel asked.

"Carl enjoys the shock you get from putting your tongue on the end of a battery."

"Is that why he's in hospital?"

"Not really. Anyway, before bringing the batteries in here, Battery Man will have rolled them between his palms, cooled them in his fridge and heated them up again in his oven. He will have left them out on the windowsill overnight and buried them in the garden. All those old wives' tales about how to get more power from your dead batteries."

"Have you ever licked a battery?" Daniel asked me.

"Only once. Didn't like it. I wouldn't recommend it."

I locked the door on the dead batteries and showed Daniel where the police stored all the yellow metal boards left over from unsolved violent crimes. There was one crime board that I suspect may have been put together in the police art department as a joke (Look at the date).

"Your birthday," Daniel said.

My son knew when my birthday was.

"Talking of dates," I said. "This is a bit macabre. Especially today." I opened another storage door to reveal enough gravestones to fill a small cemetery.

JASON THE STONEMASON

"What are they?" Daniel said.

"Works in progress," I said. "Jason the stonemason is often asked by his family and friends to carve the names of their lost loved ones onto gravestones. In the same way that if their friend was a plumber or a locksmith, they'd call him if they had a boiler that needed fixing or if they were locked out of their house I suppose.

"The trouble is. Jason feels uncomfortable taking money from his grieving family and friends at such a delicate time. And if it was someone really close to him who'd died he'd be too upset himself to carve the deceased's name into the stone without shaking. So Jason the Stonemason started engraving his stones in advance. While his family and friends are still alive. If you look through the names you'll find headstones for his wife and his mother and for many of his aunts and uncles, cousins, nephews and nieces. This one is for his sister's golden Labrador." I read the engraving out loud, "GEORGE: A TRUE AND LOYAL COMPANION." It was carved into a flawed but beautiful piece of marble for Jason's sister's not yet dead dog.

"All the stones have got names and birth dates. Some of them have got epitaphs or a few lines of poetry."

Daniel looked at the stones. Hand-cut and sandblasted, painted or gilded in white, silver and black enamel paint or gold leaf on Granite, slate and marble.

"The only thing missing on each stone is the date of death. All these headstones are here, just waiting for Jason's friends and family to die. The really sad thing is, with the rising cost of burial, the lack of sacred ground and the popularity of cremation, most of these stones will never get used. Did I ever tell you about the Evil Job Monster?"

"No." Daniel said.

"Follow me."

We went further along the corridor and I opened another door.

"Here, have a seat." I wheeled my old swivelless chair over into the room, and when Daniel was sitting as comfortably as the crappy old office chair would allow, I began.

"You know. You can tell a lot about somebody by what they choose to put into storage."

And for the first time in about twelve years, I told my son a story.

THE EVIL JOB MONSTER

"This, Daniel, is the storage unit of the Evil Job Monster," I used my Vincent Price voice. I wished I had a torch to hold under my chin. "He was a newspaper journalist who was decluttering his home. One weekend he came in carrying this rolled up carpet," I slapped an old carpet, filling the air with dust. "And he told me all about how he'd seen a list of the ten most hated professions printed in the newspaper he worked for and had decided to apply for all of them. He was going to turn the results into a newspaper story. He said he expected it to be a prize winning newspaper story."

"What was in the rolled up carpet?" Daniel asked.

"Nothing. On the list of hated occupations were traffic wardens, bouncers, estate agents, motorcycle-couriers, bus drivers, professional footballers, telesales reps, paparazzi photographers, politicians and reality TV show contestants. Some of the jobs that get you booed when you're introduced as a contestant on a TV game show. The newspaper journalist wanted to know if the people who did these jobs were really quite so terrible and if so, why? Did evil people apply for the jobs or did the jobs turn them that way? He wondered what would happen to a normal and decent human being if they took on one of these jobs. And how about if they took on all of the hated professions? The whole top ten. Would they become a monster, alienating themselves to everyone they knew and loved? He began his experiment with the number one most hated profession: traffic warden."

"Booo." Daniel said.

"Hiss," I joined in. "He issued his first ticket to a white van parked in a bus lane. He managed to write out the ticket, slip it under the windscreen wiper and make his escape before the white van man returned to the illegally parked vehicle. A tentative start, but how did he feel? Had Doctor Jekyll become Mister Hyde? The answer was no. They'd given him a uniform and he didn't think he was Hitler.

"But by the end of his first week as a traffic warden he'd ticketed over a hundred vehicles and motorists, including disabled drivers, doctors on call, school buses, cars that were parked in garages on the other side of town at the time, an ambulance and a hearse. He'd been sworn at by van drivers and taxi drivers, by ice cream men and nuns, and he'd been spat on more times than The Sex Pistols. In the evening he got a job as a bouncer."

"How do you know all this?" Daniel asked. Oh, the skepticism of youth.

"It's all in the storage," I banged the dusty carpet again. "You just have to join the dots. There's more insight to be found in an old rolled up carpet than there ever will be in the bottom of a teacup or the wrinkles of a palm."

"What was rolled up in the carpet?"

"Nothing. Anyway, the newspaperman held the heavy local nightclub doors open, welcoming the punters in with a smile, searching the handbags of the hen parties for half bottles of vodka and Coke until later, when all the good nature was poisoned with alcohol and the streets were full of staggering drunks, puking down the front of their un-tucked shirts, picking fights with passing strangers, urinating in shop doorways, putting traffic cones on their heads and showing their buttocks to anyone with a TV camera – and that was just the women. His job was to then see them on their way away from the premises without too much hoo-ha.

"Then one night, completely against character and club policy, he found himself joining in with the other doormen as they kicked a drunk man repeatedly in an alleyway. Do you want another Coke?"

"Tell the story," Daniel said.

"Alright. Next he got a job as a motorcycle courier, apparently one of the three most dangerous jobs in Britain, along with bomb disposal experts and deep-sea divers. But the reporter couldn't see what was so dangerous about it. And he couldn't see why people didn't like motorcycle messengers either. He imagined it might be because other motorists felt trapped inside their vehicles while the motorcycle couriers wove in and out of them, overtaking on the right and undertaking on the left, using bus lanes, doing wheelies at traffic lights.

"The journalist said he'd heard all about couriers kicking car wing mirrors, spitting on their windscreens and punching car bonnets but so far he personally hadn't felt the need to do any of that. The job just seemed to him to be a lot of delivering and collecting of packages and envelopes. He was tired and dirty and he was sick of eating Mars Bars because there was no time for lunch but that was about it. He hadn't even been distracted by a secretary in a short skirt on a hot day causing him to crash into the back of a bus. The worst thing about the job was that he kept dropping his bike and it weighed a ton to pick up again.

"Eventually, after dropping his bike for the fiftieth time, he just left it on the ground in a side street near Marble Arch and started walking down Oxford Street.

"Before he'd started his evil job experiment, the journey from Marble Arch to Tottenham Court Road would have taken the man about three hours: stopping for anyone who said excuse me or held out a clipboard or leaflet. He would have stopped to buy a book and a CD from the Hare Krishnas, shown a Japanese couple the way to Selfridges, answered a questionnaire about his dining and shopping habits, switched from electricity to gas and back to electricity again, bought lucky heather from a gypsy and three copies of the Big Issue. He'd set up direct debits with tabard-wearing chuggers from Save The Children and Help The Aged, and give a pound to a man playing the bagpipes.

"On the day that he abandoned his heavy motorcycle the walk along Oxford Street had taken him less than twenty minutes, during which time he'd deliberately shown a German tourist the wrong way to Baker Street, told a blind busker to shut up and asked a tramp if he had the time. His personality definitely had changed for the worse.

"The stuff he was removing from his house had changed too. He wasn't just decluttering his home anymore, he was de-humanizing it. The weekend after he abandoned his Honda he brought in all this stuff."

I showed Daniel the evidence.

"That stone Buddha there. A box of Christmas cards. One, two, three, four, five vegetarian cookbooks, a doormat with..." I turned the mat over, "the word WELCOME on and this collection of feel-good videos and DVDs. Now, what jobs are left?"

"Estate agent is next," Daniel said.

"Yes. As an estate agent the man gazumped his way to notoriety. Talking to people in a bullshit – pardon my French – glass-is-always-half-full language and making everyone hate him. It did wonders for his newspaper story. Then... What's the next job?"

"Telesales," Daniel said.

"With telesales the journalist decided to cut a few corners. He reckoned there wasn't a lot of difference between a telesales person and somebody sitting at home flicking through the phone book and ringing people up at random to annoy them. He'd save himself a lot of time doing that instead and he wouldn't have to sit in a call centre with a load of university graduates and out of work actors. The effects on his psyche would surely be the same, with his spirit just as crushed by everyone hanging up the telephone on him. During his time in telesales he put into storage…"

I showed Daniel the telltale items of the man's collapse into nastiness. "A squeeze me slowly kiss me quick hat, an I HEART NY T-shirt, a jigsaw puzzle of baked beans on toast, a lava lamp, a magic eight ball," I shook the black plastic ball, "a broken magic eight stuck on the words DON'T COUNT ON IT, and this cute photograph of himself as a baby." I showed Daniel the cute baby picture.

"Following his corner-cutting success in telesales he thought he could also save time as a paparazzi photographer if he didn't actually put any film in his camera. The part of the job that annoyed everyone was the stalking and the door-stepping. It wasn't the resulting pictures so much, as the chase across Paris," I had to stop thinking about Paris. "All he'd have to do was hang around outside Stringfellows or The Ivy with his empty camera and wait for a boyband to leave the place drunk or an actress to show him her knickers as she climbed out of a cab. He'd be finished by three in the morning and still have time to shoot across town to camp outside an unfaithful MP's wife's house and wait till morning for her to walk the dog or take the kids to school. There were six stored items from that job." I held up a copy of Queen's Greatest Hits, a novelty phone in the shape of a cartoon dog, and another photograph of the journalist as a baby.

"So far he'd found employment in… one, two, three…"

"Seven!" Daniel said, eager to get on with it.

"Yes, seven out of the UK's ten most hated professions. He'd wanted to see if it would change him for the worse, and it had." I waved a hand across the room's clutter. "As demonstrated by the contents of his storage. There were now only three jobs to go: Bus driver, reality game show gimp, and politician. All shaved monkey occupations. He should have the whole project finished and in the paper before Christmas.

"He made one final visit to his storage unit. Among the items he brought in were two Band Aid singles, a plastic Christmas tree and a cardboard box full of tinsel, baubles and fairy lights." I couldn't be bothered to clamber over to reach them so I just pointed. "They're all in that box behind the fake fish tank.

"It was on his way to his interview for the bus driver's job that he saw an unattended double-decker parked at a bus stop with its engine ticking over, awaiting a change of driver. And he stole it. In the same way that he'd cheated his way into the telesales and paparazzi jobs, he decided he could get the essence of being a bus driver a lot easier this way. He didn't need a long period of training to teach him how to put his foot hard on the accelerator as he approached a full bus stop, or to show him how to slam on the brakes when a pensioner was almost sitting down in her seat. The newspaperman climbed into the driver's cab, adjusted the height of the seat, repositioned the rearview mirror and pulled the big red cumbersome vehicle away from the kerb, swerving to run over a cat and driving straight through an estate agents window.

"He was arrested and charged with the theft of a London bus, various acts of fraud, riding a motorcycle without a license or insurance, and the attempted murder of a man outside a discotheque. He was also charged with ejecting himself from a nightclub for attempting to take a photograph of the underwear of a peer of the realm, and crashing his motorbike into the back of a bus that he had just stolen whilst being temporarily distracted by a secretary in a short skirt on a hot day. The same bus that he drove through the window of an estate agents where he himself was working at the time. These were just some of the many ways he may have come into contact with himself during what the detective who arrested him described as the most serious endangerment of the Space Time Continuum since Marty McFly in the *Back To The Future* Movies."

There was a short moment of silence, and then, even though I'd missed out a few of the jobs on the list like the footballer, the politician and the reality TV show contestant, Daniel nodded his head ever so slightly and said, "Nice story, Dad."

I could have lifted him up out of that crappy old office chair and helicoptered him around above my head till we were both dizzy and nauseous. It had taken twelve years and a room full of old household tat.

But he called me Dad.

On the way back to the office I ruffled Daniel's hair slightly and he let me do it.

Janie was outside the portacabin with her coat on. "Gary's going to drop me home, he's just gone to get something," she said. "I suddenly feel totally exhausted."

Gary came back. His parka was zipped right up to his neck. He looked even bigger than usual. I knew he'd wrapped himself in bubblewrap and hidden it under his coat. Gary the Bubblewrap Boy by name…

As Janie left she said to me, "We should talk in the morning," and she put her hand on my left cheek and I could smell the plaster cast on her arm as she kissed my ear. "Ring me. If you like. If you want."

I like. I want.

I was Johnny Depp, she was Juliette Binoche and this was the happy ending the audience had come to the cinema for. Roll credits.

I watched Janie and Gary drive off in the rattly old van. Out through the gates and off up the street. I closed the gates behind them, watching as they made their way past the new Big Yellow Storage Company that was taking shape where the kebab shop and the snooker hall used to be. I didn't care about that anymore. I didn't care if they painted *me* yellow. It had been a hell of a day. I switched the lights off, locked up and asked Daniel if he wanted to get some snacks from the most miserable sweetshop in the world on the way home.

"What do you fancy?"

"Chocolate," he said.

"Mmm, risky. But yes. I'll take that chance if you will."

"Why do you call it that, Dad? Why is it the most miserable sweetshop in the world?"

"Now there's a story. I'll tell you on the way."

"You haven't told me about the skeleton in the shoe woman's cupboard yet."

"I'll tell you that on the way too."

It was getting cold outside. The moon was there now. A new moon. It looked like Janie's smile. I turned up the collar of my crumpled suit jacket and did the same to Daniel's blazer and he didn't pull away or stop me and like a pair of Elvises we left the building.

I had definitely felt worse.

As I walked out onto the street with my son I found myself whistling like a milkman. Whistling like a man who, although he'd been up since four in the morning driving a rickety electric van, knew that his working day would nearly be over and he'd be tucked up in a warm bed or in the pub by elevenses. It was the whistle of a man who could hold up to a dozen empty milk bottles between the fingers of one hand. A man who'd be doing it in the afternoon with lonely housewives in see-thru negligees while their unsuspecting husbands were at work earning money to pay for his Christmas tip.

My whistle that evening was a Tom Good from *The Good Life* type of whistle. The actual tune I was whistling didn't exist until I'd started whistling it. Without thinking about it I was writing a song. It would be the second track on my comeback album. Track two after my Janie song, which had now taken on a whole new meaning and significance. My whistling song might need a verse and a middle eight or a shift from minor to major, something for the boybands to get off their stools for when they covered it. It might even be a duet. I wondered if Janie could sing.

As Daniel and me were halfway down dogshit alley, just past the gnats, with me still whistling like Richard Briers, I was mugged. My attackers showed me a sharp object – perhaps it twinkled in the moonlight – and they told me to give them something to help them on their journey or they'd cut me, or worse still they'd *cut the fucking kid*. Their hands were already in my pockets searching through all my loose change, bus tickets, trouser fluff and tissues before I could work out how to react. Going through my pockets with all the skill and dexterity of street magicians removing my braces for the amusement of a TV audience, they produced a small brown envelope and opened it.

"What the fuck is *this?* What's this Mickey fucking Mouse shit?"

Carl's Scottish fivers.

"Is it fucking toy money?"

"No. It's real," I said.

"Fucking foreign money."

"No, seriously. Small shops won't take it but you can use it in the supermarket or change it at a bank." My head was bobbing up and down with nerves like a dog on a spring in the back of a car. I was babbling like an idiot and grovelling like a pathetic coward. And in front of my son. A pathetic nodding cowardly dog. Scooby fucking Doo.

"Dad?" Daniel said to me, using my informal noun for the third time in one night. He wanted me to deal with this situation like a proper dad.

I should have just given them everything I had and they would have been on their way, like Dick Turpin and his swashbuckling chum the *Gentleman Highwayman*. I should have just let the gentlemen highwaymen do their job. All this Scottish currency being legal tender nonsense was going to do none of us any good.

"Are you taking the fucking piss? Where's your money?" one of the boys – because that's what they were, probably not a lot older than Daniel – said.

"Cut him."

"Give us your phone."

"I haven't got a phone."

"We'll fucking stab you, give us something."

"I haven't got anything, only the Scottish money and my watch, take that. It's not brilliant. It's a fucking shit fucking watch." Now I was offering them stuff they hadn't asked for and I was swearing a lot so that I might somehow fit in. Trying to be a social chameleon. If I appeared more like them, maybe they wouldn't kill me. For half a stupid Mickey Mouse second I considered asking them if they knew who I was. Like if they thought I was a celebrity they might let me off. As though being famous might be the same as wearing glasses or being a girl. If I gave them my autograph and posed for an out-of-focus mobile phone picture that would be the end of it. They could sell it on ebay. Famous people didn't get mugged.

Before I had the chance, they took my Mickey Mouse watch and Carl's Mickey Mouse money, and that should really have been the end of it but it was actually just the beginning.

It started with a kiss. A Glasgow Kiss as valid in England as Carl's Scottish pound notes. The head butt knocked me backwards and then – physics are a peculiar thing – forwards again, fixing my broken nose for five thousand pounds less than a Harley Street doctor had once quoted me. Every cloud…

A whole world of trouble followed.

From the Glasgow kiss it was on to Hong Kong for some Fancy Dan Kung Fu kicks, back across the globe to the East End of London for a few bare knuckle punches, and then abroad once more and also back in time for the cut and thrust of a musketeer's blade from 17th century France. A world tour of international dirty fight moves that would have had the Marquis of Queensbury turning over and over in his grave had he not been cremated in Woking in 1900. More useless fucking information from the World Wide Web.

I didn't scream or cry out for help, and once I was on the ground I just lay there and took my kicking like the man I should have been in the first place. In a funny way it was almost a relief to get it all over and done with. All the time I was on the ground, wishing it had been me instead of Gary who'd stuffed his jacket with bubblewrap, I looked up at my son and I wanted to cry but he seemed to be crying enough for both of us.

Eventually my attackers grew bored with my lack of participation and stopped. They both spat on me and then climbed onto children's bicycles and disappeared into the early evening darkness, chucking wheelies and laughing as they went.

When they were gone I picked myself up from the ground. I was covered in blood, footprints, tears and snot and feeling like a cunt. I spat some blood onto my shoe and groaned to my son,

"Come on Daniel. Before they come back."

We started walking back the way we'd come. No whistling this time. I doubted I'd ever whistle again.

Back at the portacabin I tried to calm Daniel down. Everything was all right. Daddy wasn't dying. It looked a lot worse than it was. This was what they meant on the television when they talked about superficial wounds. Not deep. A knife had been used on me but I'd been jabbed rather than stabbed. I wished there was more blood.

I phoned a cab to take us home. I made Daniel some toast and Marmite and went to the bathroom to put a plaster on my deepest knife cut, the one that might have needed a stitch or two if I was going to go to a hospital, which I wasn't. I stared at my bloody self in the bathroom mirror. I guess I looked hard now. I didn't feel it. I stopped staring because I was making myself cry. I went back downstairs and sat with Daniel while he moved beans and toast around his plate. We both sat in silence until Daniel started crying again, his tears dripping onto his beans. I wanted to comfort him but I couldn't really remember how. My son had been such a stranger to me for so long that when I touched him I felt more like a pervert than a concerned father. I started crying as well.

I'd never wanted to bond with him quite this much.

And what was his mother going to say?

She'd be sleeping now. Full of Merlot and expensive French food, softly snoring garlic and grape breaths onto the tanned and hairy back of her new man. I bet Julian was a real man. Karen would be sleeping soundly in her hotel bed after their romantic evening together. Sleeping soundly in the knowledge that her son's father hadn't taken her little boy to a funeral and got himself drunk, had sex in a toilet with the grieving widow and then rounded the night off by getting himself beaten up by children in a shit-covered alleyway on the way to the sweetshop while his son watched and cried.

I took Daniel up to my room; he got undressed, and took his backpack off – why hadn't he used his parachute? He lay on the bed and I covered him with a blanket and he was asleep almost immediately. I sat with him for a while, watching him breathe and then I went back downstairs and made a bed for myself on the sofa.

I couldn't sleep.

There was a song going round and round in my aching head. It was stuck on the third verse and I couldn't seem to make it to the end of the verse and onto the second chorus, to the middle eight and the final chorus, so that the song could fade out and let me sleep. It's what bedtime must be like for an ice cream man trying to sleep after a long hot day of *Popeye The Sailor Man* over and over again.

I woke in the middle of the night and had to get quickly upstairs to the toilet to throw up. As I retched and groaned into the toilet bowl, my eyes watering and sweat pouring from my brow, I could taste the evening's fruity communist alcohol, and the toilet water looked like Um Bongo. That made me throw up again, until there was nothing left to come up, except my spleen, my lungs, my kidneys and what was left of my soul.

On the way back from the bathroom I checked that Daniel was still asleep. Like I'd done when he was a baby. Checking for heartbeat movement in the blankets. Never trusting the baby monitor. I wondered if he was dreaming now. Having a nightmare about his cowardly dad.

I got a red plastic bucket from under the kitchen sink in case I was sick again and went back to the sofa and eventually I drifted off. I dreamt that somebody was inflating a balloon inside my head. The balloon kept growing. I was walking along the street and small children were screwing their faces up, because they could see the skin of my face was soon going to get so thin that it would burst. And then the balloon and my face both exploded. There were bits of latex rubber and my face on the pavement. A dog wandered over and ate a piece of burst balloon that was stuck to a piece of my burst cheek and he started to choke on it, causing him to vomit. Then the dog instinctively re-ate the bits of balloon and my face that he'd just sicked up, only to gag once more and puke again. And that's the way it went on. Even though my face was in bits on the ground and in the dog's belly I could still see that disgusting dog puking and eating, eating and puking. And it would have gone on forever. Until somebody threw him a stick or a ball, or he caught sight of his own tail or a wasp or a butterfly distracted his attention away from my sicked-up face. Or until I woke up or moved on to another nightmare.

When I next woke it was the afternoon and I had somebody else's face, a big fat misshapen ugly mess. The blood and snot that had come out of my nose and mouth had congealed and I looked like I'd been flanned with jam sponge cakes on *Tiswas,* or like a pizza that had fallen off the back of the delivery boy's moped. I had to peel my sticky cheek away from the sofa cushion. I cleaned some of the dried blood away from my face. Every part of my body ached. My jaw felt like it was on upside-down and my cheek was swollen to the size of half a watermelon. I guessed that everyone would call me Melon Head from now on.

I emptied the red bucket into the toilet and flushed the frothy colourful liquid away. I'd never drink again.

Daniel was in the front room watching television. The same programme I'd seen not long ago about the couple moving to Cornwall. It seemed like a pretty good idea now.

I spent the day indoors with my son. Him watching videos and reading, and me tentatively dabbing at my injuries with a wet flannel and trying to find something I could eat without too much pain. I'd probably go to the doctor or the hospital tomorrow. I couldn't tell how much of my pain was from the kicking and how much was a hangover and I didn't want to be accused of wasting NHS time.

I didn't call the police; what was the point? If I were to see any of my attackers again I wouldn't recognise them. I couldn't pick them out of a line up. It all happened so quickly, it was dark, I wasn't paying attention, I'd been drinking, they were wearing hoods. They'd just suddenly been there in front of me and then I was on the ground and then they were gone. They weren't dressed up as cowboys or pirates. They didn't have spider's web tattoos on their faces, they weren't wearing eye patches, they didn't have hooks for hands or curly ginger haircuts.

If I did go to the police they'd want to drive me round the most frightening part of town to see if I could spot my attackers. They'd shove Daniel and me in the back of their attention-seeking car with POLICE written down the side and a blue flashing light on the top. They might as well drive us round in a car with my name and home address written down the side of it instead. Have a helicopter fly overhead beaming down a bright spotlight that spelled out the words **THEY ARE HERE**.

Like the arrow on the bus shelter map that the music journalist lied about.

The police would then expect me to get out of the car and identify my attackers so they'd know exactly who *I* was. Then after they were let off on a technicality or with a caution and a fifteen-pound fine they could come round to my house and finish the job off. Making sure I knew just before they delivered the final deathblow that they were going to kill my child next.

The best I could hope for from such ace modern detective work would be a quick return to fame. To have my age, description and crime genre printed onto a yellow police crime board. And we all know where they end up.

"The police won't make this any better, Dan," I said to Daniel as if he'd just suggested it to me.

"I know, Dad."

"I should tell your mum, though. I'll wait till she gets back from France. Don't you think?" I knew if I rang Karen she'd panic. Get the next plane home and then I'd probably never be allowed to see Daniel ever again. "No need to ruin her holiday with Jonathan."

"Julian," Daniel corrected me, even though I think he knew that I really knew the name of Karen's new man.

I needed to tell Janie too, even if it was just so I could ask her to go to work and open up for me until I felt less like the Elephant Man and was ready to face the public again. But I didn't want to spoil Janie's holiday either. She had a few days off for bereavement leave. Time she planned to spend burning her dead husband's belongings on a big bonfire and to go lingerie shopping. Even with the pain and shame I was suffering I still managed a slight erection at the thought of that – God was having a right old laugh when he created man in his image. I decided to leave Janie to her pants shopping and bonfire burning.

The person I wanted to tell most was Carl. But I didn't want to take Daniel to the psychiatric hospital with me and I wasn't going to leave him home alone. I wasn't completely sure what I'd had stolen. There may have been something with my home address on. As I watched the television couple moving to Cornwall carry a sofa into a big yellow building I decided I'd tell everyone later.

Later that day I cooked Daniel my signature dish of more baked beans on toast, this time with grated cheese on the top. I filled a plate with just the soft grated cheese for myself and, between tentative and painful bites, I told Daniel all about Imelda's shoes and the skeleton she found when she cleared them all out of her wardrobe. The story I was going to tell him before I was so rudely interrupted in dogshit alley. Because I really just needed to talk.

The Skeleton in Imelda's Closet

Walter was impatient. He was impetuous. Walter wouldn't and couldn't wait for anything. He could never have waited as long as Daniel had waited to hear about the skeleton in Imelda's shoe closet. Walter simply couldn't have waited. He would have found it impossible.

When Walter bought a new book he always had to read the last paragraph first. He couldn't bear to commit himself to tens of thousands of words without knowing what the last hundred were going to be. He had to know where it was all leading to before he started reading. Precipitous is another Walter word. When the weathermen forecast precipitation, they were warning us that Walter was in town. Better take an umbrella. Wear something Walter-proof.

Walter was one of those people who couldn't enjoy a film or a television programme without knowing how it ended first. And once he did know, he had to let everybody else know as well. He ruined the endings of many films for his friends by telling them who the killer was or who died or lived happily ever after. Happily ever after, that was Walter's favourite ending. He liked the girl got, the baddies killed and the hero riding off into the sunset, preferably with the words THE END filling the centre of the cinema screen.

Walter never really enjoyed a film until he saw it for the second time, which was when he'd sit back and ruin it for everybody who was seeing it for the first time, laughing just before the joke that he knew was coming or telling the punch line to a joke that somebody else up onscreen was only in the middle of, or taking a tissue from his pocket just before the movie's pivotal sad and tragic scene. Walter spoiled many cinema trips for his friends by giving away the ending, and he did the same for them with television programmes and books. Walter ruined everything. He was a pathological spoilsport. And yes, he spoiled sport as well.

He'd tell people football scores they didn't want to know because they'd videoed the highlights, or how such and such boxer gets knocked out in the first round.

If Walter was alive today, whenever the announcer at the end of a TV series gave the viewer the option of *switching over to another channel now* to see next week's episode, Walter could never have waited, he'd always have had to switch over. He didn't like inconclusive or open endings to anything; he preferred closure or whatever it was called when Walter was still alive. He hated cliffhangers and he didn't like uncertainty. One of the last films Walter saw before he died was the one we'd named our business after. Poor Walter almost imploded at the ambiguous ending of that sci-fi classic.

If Walter was alive today he'd subscribe to all those celebrity gossip magazines that tell you what's going to happen in soap operas before it actually does. He'd watch breakfast television just for the soap opera spoilers. *Look away now* on the football results at the end of the news meant exactly the opposite to Walter.

When he was a child, Walter's parents had to hide his Christmas and birthday presents at a friend's house to stop their son from finding and opening them early. He'd be the worst secret Santa in the office where he worked later in life. Walter couldn't wait until Christmas to discover what he was getting from *his* secret Santa and he also had to tell whoever he'd been picked to buy a present for what it was he'd bought them. He'd then go on to tell everybody else in the office what they'd be getting as well; he was more Overt Santa than secret. Wrapping paper and the effort of wrapping an awkward shaped gift was all wasted on Walter, just chuck it in a see-thru bag.

When a letter landed on Walter's doormat he couldn't open it until he'd first worked out who it was from and what it was, struggling to decipher the half stamped postmark and holding the envelope up to the light to see what was inside. Walter couldn't do a newspaper crossword unless the answers were printed upside down on page 49. His least favourite chocolates were Revels.

After years of ruining all their surprise birthday parties, a group of Walter's friends decided the only way to keep the next big surprise party a secret was to kidnap Walter. To tie him up, gag him and lock him in the wardrobe of the house where they were holding the party. And then, after they'd shouted *Surprise!* and sung happy birthday, they could go and unlock the wardrobe and – as Michael Palin might have said in *The Life Of Brian* – release Walter.

They'd cut the sticky tape and the ropes and apologise to Walter and hope he'd understand their seemingly extreme actions. They'd kiss his sticky lips and return to the party together. That was the plan.

The next big surprise party was looming. Walter's friends hired a coach to make sure everyone would turn up at the party together and make the surprise a really big one. The first successful surprise party they'd thrown since meeting Walter.

As the coach approached a busy roundabout the driver appeared to lose control of the vehicle. Eyewitnesses said they watched it career across the icy road, overturning and rolling down the side of a hill. There were no survivors.

The man whose surprise party it was presumed that all his friends had forgotten his birthday; not even his sister had bothered to turn up to the pub where she said she'd meet him, having planned to then take him unsuspectingly on to the surprise house party.

It was uncertain, the exact cause of Walter's death. When he was found in the wardrobe, it was a bit late for forensics; by then it was more of a job for an archaeologist. A combination of suffocation and shock was most likely what finally did for him. Tied up in such a confined space with carpet tape across his mouth must have made it difficult for him to breathe, and he would have struggled to try and free himself. Judging by the position of his skeleton, his struggling had left him wedged face down with his knees tucked under his chin, which would have led Walter to positional asphyxia, or postural asphyxia – take your pick, they're both the same thing.

Shock played its part in Walter's demise too. The experience of being bound and gagged in your friend's wardrobe for no apparent reason, not knowing what was happening or why or when it was all going to end. Such a never-ending mystery story must have been enough to kill somebody like Walter all by itself.

There was nobody there to pound on Walter's chest or shock him back to life. His friends were all dead at the bottom of a ditch in a mangled coach with no seatbelts. No one called an ambulance. Nobody had to make any tough decisions about whether to turn off any life support machines; no one had to sign a tear stained release form. There was nobody there to put Walter out of his misery; he went all the way through that alone, from misery start to misery finish, tied up in a cupboard. Perhaps he saw his whole life flashing before him; at least he would have known exactly what would happen in that particular movie.

Walter's body began to destroy itself. Dropping in temperature as his internal sphincter muscles relaxed, his blood moved to the lowest parts of the body and within thirty minutes it had started to coagulate. If Walter had been discovered around about this time and his body moved there would have been a release of urine, faeces and undigested food – who'd be an ambulance man or an undertaker?

Walter's muscles would have stiffened with rigor mortis, peaking at about twelve hours after death and relaxing again another twenty four hours later. Within a day Walter's remains would be under attack from bacteria, fungi, beetles, ants and wasps and other scavengers. Internally, the structure of his maggot-ravaged body began to collapse. Walter was eating himself. The bacterial action created gases, causing his body to bloat and swell, stinking out the empty house. And then his skin fell off.

Walter became a skeleton.

And he stayed there locked in the cupboard in his floor-to-ceiling fitted coffin. The house remained empty and unsold for years after its owner died in the coach tragedy. The FOR SALE sign fell over into the front garden and the weeds and grass grew over it. Walter's remains remained. As 1985 went on around him and without him, Walter would have missed Mikhail Gorbachev becoming Soviet leader and Mohammed Al Fayed buying Harrods. He'd miss Hulk Hogan and Mr. T taking part in Wrestlemania (Walter's favourite sport as the outcome was always a foregone conclusion) at Madison Square Garden, and the launch of *New Coke*. Walter also missed the Greenpeace ship Rainbow Warrior being sunk by French spies, and South Africa ending its ban on interracial marriages.

Walter would miss Status Quo and Queen, Bob Geldof and Bono, all performing for Live Aid at Wembley Stadium. In the first year that Walter wasn't found, Nazi *Angel of Death* Josef Mengele *was*. Nazi hunters found Mengele's body in Brazil and they dug it up.

Two sunken ships were found: The Titanic was located two miles southeast of the suitably named Newfoundland. The Spanish galleon Nuestra Senora de Atocha was found along with four hundred million dollars worth of silver and coins at the bottom of the ocean off the Florida Keys.

Walter was not found.

In that first year in the wardrobe he missed out on ruining the endings of the movies *The Breakfast Club, Back To The Future* and *Witness*.

Among those joining Walter in Heaven that year were Rock Hudson, Ricky Nelson and Orson Welles. While Keira Knightley, Jack (son of Ozzy) Osbourne and the chubby footballer Wayne Rooney were all born to take their place on Earth.

In 1986 new estate agents took over the property where Walter lay. They had it painted in wall-to-wall Magnolia and a fitted kitchen was fitted but still no sale. The first people to view the house thought there was a smell about the place, "like someone's died," they said. New carpets were put in and removed again. The floorboards were stripped, varnished and then ripped up and replaced with laminated MDF. Walter's wardrobe itself changed colour from Brilliant White to White With a Hint of Apple and then back to Magnolia like the walls of the second bedroom it was screwed and glued into. Nobody looked inside the wardrobe because it was locked and the key lost amongst the wreckage of the crashed coach.

It took ten years to eventually sell the house – to Imelda and her husband, who had to break the wardrobe lock with a hammer and chisel to get the door open so he could throw his wife's ludicrous amount of shoes in. He didn't look. He just poured them in like he was delivering coal.

When I finally made it to the A & E department it was a lot more like the Hogarth Insane Asylum I'd expected to find Carl committed to. There were more mad people in A & E than there were on Carl's ward. People were arguing, throwing up blood on the lino, undoing their stitches in fresh fights and abusing the nurses. A man in a torn and bloody shirt ran through the hospital reception chased by an overweight and out of breath security guard. The bandage covering half the man's face had come unravelled and a nurse put her foot on one end of it until it wrapped round his neck and almost garrotted him. It gave the security guard time to catch up and wrestle the man to the floor in a puddle of mostly his own blood. The police arrived and the man was taken back into the hospital for re-bandaging.

"Novel way to jump the queue," I said to Daniel, and gave him some money to get something from the drinks machine, which turned out to be broken. The fist-shaped dent in the middle of the word Pepsi may have been the cause. I thought the lump on my face would slot into the dent in the drink machine almost perfectly.

In reception a nurse came and took my details. She looked like Hattie Jacques. I had difficulty suppressing an *Oooh matron* Kenneth Williams impression. She got me to fill in a form. I wrote down my name and address, the name of my GP, my date of birth and the cause of my accident and emergency, and then Hattie Jacques told me to take a seat until I was called.

After an hour's wait a different nurse called out my name and showed me and Daniel to another room where we sat on different uncomfortable chairs and waited another fifty minutes until an Eastern European student doctor or nurse – I wasn't sure which – came to see me and once again noted my postcode, the name of my GP, my date of birth and the cause of my accident and emergency.

As we sat and waited for the next doctor to take my details, Daniel and me created Goth Cop lookalike photo-fits of some of the other patients.

Sitting opposite was a girl with a nosebleed. She was holding a towel against the blood flow and she had her head tilted back. When the blood slowed to a drip she removed the towel to reveal an uncanny spiky-haired likeness to Toyah Wilcox. Daniel didn't know who Toyah Wilcox was and thought she looked more like David Bowie in *Labyrinth*.

Toyah was sitting between a woman whom Daniel thought looked a little bit like Sylvester Stallone, and a man in a green army jacket who probably thought he looked like Robert De Niro in *Taxi Driver* but really just looked like a bloke in an army jacket with a bad Mohican haircut.

A male nurse swung through the thick plastic swing doors. The doors looked like dirty Edam cheese. The nurse was carrying an armful of patients' medical records and he called half-heartedly for a Mister O-somebody-or-other like he didn't care whether or not he found him. He whisper-called the name about three and a half times and then went back through the cheese swing doors. The male nurse reminded both Daniel and me of the male nurse Charlie in the TV show *Casualty*; it might have just been the uniform and the location.

"I wonder what came first?" I said to Daniel. "Did he go for the job because he already looked like Britain's most famous male nurse or did he look different when he started the job and was it the job itself that was slowly turning him into Charlie Fairhead?" The same applied to Hattie Jacques.

The celebrity photo-fitting was making my face throb.

A young black man was over by the reception desk demonstrating to a nurse the angle of the punch that had led to his wounded hand and it struck me that this could have been one of my attackers. A work-related injury.

That was when I realised I had another wound that I hadn't noticed before. It hurt more than all the cuts and contusions. It was more painful and ugly and less superficial than the bruised ribs, the fat melon head or the wonky jaw.

Watching the young man having his hand examined, keeping my head bowed in case he recognised me as one of his victims, I realised that after beginning the week as an open-minded liberal, the writer of all those albums full of impassioned political songs, the man the music press came to for a quote about the rise of the far right. The poster boy for political pop: all over the music press, shouting into a megaphone beneath the anti-Nazi banner at the front of a march entering Hyde Park. After starting the week free from bigotry my woolly liberalism was unravelling. My Starsky cardigan had shrunk to an Alf Garnett tank top. I was just another racist. I felt like writing a song about myself and organising a benefit gig to stop me from spreading my vile hatred.

Charlie Fairhead came through the cheese doors. He looked down at a thin folder of notes and mumbled my name.

While I was having my face and ribs x-rayed the radiologist asked me if I was that guy. And I said, what guy? And she asked me if I'd been on television and I said that I had. She asked me if I was a singer and I told her I was and this went on for a while until we finally reached the end of our twenty questions game and the radiologist made a joke about me signing my x-rays and how she was going to put them on ebay. If my sides weren't already split they certainly had now. Thank God I was in a hospital.

I thought of the old saying about whether a tree falling in a deserted forest made a sound when there was nobody there to hear it. I thought about what the barmaid had pointed out at the wake. I wondered whether, if people needed to ask if I was famous, was I famous at all? I could have boasted to the doctor about how I'd had my fair share of hit records and how I'd topped the charts back in my day. I could have carried photographs and newspaper clippings around with me to show to people when they asked if I used to be a star. Pictures of me on stage at huge festivals with sixty thousand people with their arms in the air, braving the mud and rain and spending a month's wages to clap along with a song I wrote. I could have carried my gold discs around with me as proof of my fame.

If I needed to provide proof of my fame though, did it really exist? I didn't want to boast about my fame. I wanted everyone to just know.

As I left, the radiologist said to the mother of a small boy with a broken arm,

"He's a pop star, you know."

And I had to sign the boy's sling with his mother's lipstick. I said no to the mobile phone picture though, using the fact that you aren't allowed to use mobiles in the hospital as my excuse for her not photographing my fat head.

I sat with Daniel in one more waiting room until a nurse brought me my injury results. I had a bruised but not broken rib, two fractured cheekbones and a misaligned jaw. There was good news: my hearing problem seemed to have disappeared. This was a second layer of silver lining. The blows to my face and head had not only straightened my nose but had also fixed my hearing problem. You'd think that I'd been beaten up by doctors.

I left the hospital with an appointment card for the maxillofacial unit, a bottle of strong painkillers and as a racist. I hoped that last wound wouldn't scar. I took Daniel back to his mother.

"What in Christ's name happened to your face?" Karen said.

"I know. I look like a melon," I said. "And it turns out I'm a racist."

"What?"

Karen hadn't been home long. She was still dressed in the designer clothes she'd bought on her Paris love trip. She smelled of French perfume and if my sense of smell had been keener I expect I would have also been able to smell the entrées and the aperitifs. The Brioche, the Croque Monsieur, the café au lait and the sex.

"Are *you* alright, Danny? What happened?" Karen said, scooping her son towards her and away from his dangerous dad. She gave Daniel a quick once over for any signs of external injuries. "Go inside. I'll be in in a minute."

Daniel said goodbye to me and went inside. Karen turned back to me. "You look awful. Have you been to the hospital? What in Christ's name happened?"

I told her the full story. Not the full story. I left out the details of the Russian alcopops and the toilet and Janie. I compensated for the missing information by adding a few bits of my own creation. I doubled the age and number of my attackers. I exaggerated my injuries and the pain I was in and also the relaxed way I was dealing with it all.

"What did they say at the hospital?"

"I've got a few broken ribs," (more than was actually true, and broken now rather than simply bruised), "two fractured cheekbones, a misaligned jaw and a lot of other bruising." (I completely made that last part up.) "They gave me some painkillers. The man in the hospital pharmacy suggested that I speed up the effects of the tablets by masturbating."

"*What?*"

"He said it sends the drugs quicker to your head. In your

blood or something."

"That's outrageous."

"I know. I'm not particularly in a sexy mood either. Do you think I should report him to, I don't know, the matron or somebody? To Hattie Jacques?"

"You should go home. You're rambling," Karen said.

"I will," I said.

I wished I didn't need to exaggerate. I almost would have preferred it if my injuries had been more severe. Something that required a life-saving operation. My attackers should have kicked a bit harder. Why can't people do their jobs properly anymore? Why wasn't I in a coma for God's sake? Karen and Janie could take turns keeping vigil by my hospital bedside, holding my hand and talking to me about the good times. Playing me my favourite songs and reading me my get well soon cards, both of them hoping they'd be the one to see me wake from my deep sleep and ask for a cold pint of beer and a bucket of Kentucky Fried Chicken.

I gave Karen Daniel's bag with his books and his screwed-up school clothes and his parachute that had failed to open. For a moment we both had our hands on the rucksack and I saw the woman that I'd once fallen in love with and I wanted to say something about that. I remembered how I used to think she looked like Julia Roberts. How had I managed to trick two such attractive Hollywood lookalikes into falling for a racist has-been with a face like a large fruit? I just said, "Goodbye."

And I went to bust Carl out of the loony bin.

At the bus station they were trying out a combination of violins, safety announcements and psychology to keep the young and the troublesome under control. The announcements came at regular intervals.

"Skateboarding, cycling and ball games are not allowed anywhere in the bus station. Thank you. Please keep all baggage and belongings with you at all times. Any unattended items may be removed and destroyed."

The announcements created the illusion that we were being watched. As though help was close at hand, watching a TV monitor in a nearby room. The Bomb Squad, the skateboard police, all ready to drop like rain through the ceiling of the bus station. Abseiling to our rescue to defuse the unattended luggage and save us from impending bus station peril at the hands of drug crazed munchkins.

There was nobody watching.

No one to save us. We were alone.

The gentle classical tunes that filled the building were

there to confuse the teenagers who didn't like the stuffy music. There was no beat and there weren't any lyrics and it made them nervous. Why was classical music playing in the bus station? Who was playing the music? It freaked them out. And so they waited outside in the rain where they couldn't hear it.

The bus station music came from one those classical hits albums with titles like *20 Classical Chill Out Tunes* and *Relax With The Classics*. While I waited for my bus the music reminded me of old television adverts and of more innocent times.

To me *Air On The G String* was the theme tune to those hilarious Hamlet Cigars TV adverts from the 1970s and 80s, and Tchaikovsky's *The Nutcracker Suite* I knew with the words *He's a Cadburys Fruit and Nut case, crazy for those Cadbury's nuts and raisins*. I think *Pachelbel's Canon in D Major* had once tried to sell me *Pure New Wool* and it also reminded me of getting drunk and dancing to *Go West*, the Village People's version of the tune. *Ponchielli's Dance of the Hours* transported me back to my first trip to the cinema to see *Fantasia*. It made me think about cartoon hippos and elephants wearing tutus.

The last two pieces of bus station musak I heard before my bus came were Ravel's *Bolero*, which made me think of Christopher Dean throwing Jane Torvill across the rink like she was a rag doll at the Winter Olympics, and then, as my bus arrived, the start of the *O Fortuna* chorus from Carmina Burana. The music from *The Omen*! The scariest tune ever written! Satan's theme tune! Exactly how chilled out and relaxed was that supposed to make all the timid old cuppachino and soft biscuit ladies and sensitive victims like me feel, Mister bus station man?

The bus pulled up and I found a seat on the lower deck at the back. I brushed a couple of French fries and a screwed up burger wrapper onto the floor and picked up a newspaper somebody had left behind. On the front page it said, *EARTHQUAKE IN SOUTH EAST ASIA – THOUSANDS DEAD*. An international news story of such gigantic and far away tragedy that I could just turn the page and look at a half dressed tart in a hardhat holding a spanner without feeling too distraught. It was the local newspaper stories that upset me. Even more than before, now that I was just one more hapless victim of local crime.

All those local newspapers that had accumulated under my kitchen sink beneath the red sick bucket. All chock-full of scary local news. Too scary. Too local. I was fine *with EARTHQUAKE IN SOUTH EAST ASIA* or *WAR IN MIDDLE EAST. FIFTEEN PUPILS DEAD IN FLORIDA SCHOOL SHOOTING* wasn't going to affect my day. All that news was far away. Like the stuff on the Nine O'clock News that I could just let wash over me without it ruining the comedy programme and good night's sleep that followed it.

INTERNATIONAL TERROIST GROUP HAVE NUCLEAR WEAPON.

ASTEROID WILL HIT EARTH.

It was practically fantasy fiction.

The stories on the front pages of my local newspaper were real. Close by and real. *PENSIONER BEATEN WITH A HAMMER,* they informed me. Beaten with a hammer in the car park opposite my workplace. *RANDOM KNIFE ATTACKS OUT OF CONTROL,* they said. Out of control in the shopping centre where I did my Christmas shopping. And random too, that most terrifying of crime words. Crazy people not killing their own. I read *GANG THREATENS TWIN BABIES OF HEAVILY PREGNANT MOTHER,* and it was the fact that she was threatened in the flats I walked through every day to reach my house that scared me so.

I closed the paper and folded it back onto the seat next to me. I had newsprint ink on my hands. The ink of a thousand earthquake victims. I thought of Macbeth.

Resting my face against the bus window, I swallowed the lump that had been growing in my throat over the course of the day and let the cold glass of the filthy bus window sooth my swollen cheek for a while. When the bus hit a bump in the road, braked suddenly or lowered with a ssshhh to let a pensioner climb aboard with her wheeled shopping basket, I banged my face on the glass. I winced with pain and then rested my cheek again to feel the cool of the glass on my hot wound. Through the dirty bus window I watched the world go by.

In the hospital's entrance hall I phoned Janie. I couldn't get my head far enough inside the plastic dome around the payphone that was stuck to the wall to feel like speaking freely, so I whispered.

"Hello? What is it?" Janie said. "I can't hear you. Can you speak up?"

I spoke a bit louder. "I'm going to be in late today. I haven't been in to work since the funeral. Could you go and open up?"

"What's happened? Are you ill? You sound strange"

I thought about telling her I'd fallen down the stairs, maybe into a door. But that was her lie so she'd know I was lying too.

"I was attacked. Mugged."

"By who? When? Where?"

"On the way home. The other night. Just a couple of kids, pathetic really."

"How badly hurt are you?"

"Not too bad. Bruised ribs, fractured cheekbones and my jaw's in the wrong place. I can't eat. Except for mashed potato and I had some grated cheese. My ear is better though and I think my nose is straighter. People pay for this sort of stuff."

"Are you at the hospital?"

"No. Yes. No. Well, I've been to the hospital but now I'm at the other hospital. The one where Carl is."

"Did you report it?"

"No."

"Maybe you should report it."

"I'd feel a bit stupid doing it now. I've left it too late. Janie, I think I'm a racist now." I was whispering again.

"You're a what?"

I virtually put the phone's receiver in my mouth and I whispered again, "Racist. I'm a racist." I seemed to be admitting the fact to more people than anyone from the BNP ever did. Maybe I wasn't a proper racist after all.

An Asian woman walked past just at the right time to hear me whispering the word racist loudly into the hospital payphone. It was the doctor who looked like the actress from *ER* and *Bend it Like Beckham*. As she walked passed she gave a half smile hello.

I nodded my acknowledgement and turned back to whisper into the phone, "Can I tell you when I see you?"

"Okay," Janie suddenly realised something. "Oh my God, was Daniel there?"

"Where?"

"When you were mugged."

"Yes."

"Oh my God."

"He's alright. They didn't touch him. He's with Karen. I doubt she'll let me see him again. I'm going to have to get the Batman suit and climbing ropes out of the cleaners."

"What? Are you on drugs?"

"Ibuprofen. The chemist told me to..." I leaned right into the phone space helmet to whisper the word *masturbate* but thought better of it. "I'll tell you that when I see you as well."

"What are you going to do now?"

"Go see Carl. Do you hate me?"

"Why would I hate you?"

"I don't know."

"Ring me after you've seen Carl. And give him my love." I contemplated a number of different answers to that:

1. Coarse – "What, in the hospital toilet?"

2. Greedy – "I want all your love for myself."

There was a third but the money ran out and I didn't have any more change and the line went dead.

Monday at the psychiatric hospital was haircut and nails day. Every Monday a hairdressing and beauty salon would be set up on the ward. The female patients would get any fingernails they hadn't already bitten off trimmed, filed, buffed, polished and painted. Patients could get a free makeover. A new haircut for a new beginning.

Carl had been made over. He was clean-shaven, making his exposed lips look strangely pursed. Like they were someone else's lips. His eyebrows had started to grow back making him look less alien though. He was still wearing his greasy red hat but when I walked in he made a show of removing it to reveal his almost cleanly shaved head. I looked for lobotomy scars or dimples on his temples from the ECT electrodes. I couldn't see either. It was just a haircut. I looked for life behind his eyes, beyond his bottle-thick glasses that with his new haircut made Carl look like somebody. I thought at first it was Elvis Costello but Elvis Costello had more hair. I was growing sick of constantly seeing other people in everyone. I blamed the Goth Cop and wished I'd chosen a different mobile library book. If I'd picked the self-surgery one instead, Carl might never have ended up here.

Carl had also been over the road to the dental hospital since my last visit to have his teeth fixed. His lisp was gone. Overall, he looked in a lot better shape than me.

"Woah. What happened to you?"

"I know. I look like a watermelon."

"I was thinking more honeydew myself."

He was right. My melon head would continue to change size and colour for another two weeks. The Casualty doctor had told me that. She didn't use the melon family as a frame of reference, but over the next couple of weeks my face would change from Watermelon to Honeydew and then – not the Gala melon shade you might have expected – but the yellowy brown of a pumpkin or more accurately: baby shit. Everyone could call me Pumpkin Face. They could hollow my head out every 31st of October and stick lighted candles inside my skull. Or maybe I'd have the nickname Babyshitface for the rest of my life instead.

I told Carl about the mugging. This time I told the truth. Not the simple somebody hit me that I'd told the doctors and nurses, or the embellished macho nonsense that I'd told my ex-wife to make me appear a heroic victim. The only thing I left out for Carl was the Scottish fivers. I didn't want Carl to think I was blaming him somehow.

When I told him all about Janie, he said, "I knew. I always knew."

"How did you know? You didn't know. How did you know?"

"I think she did too. It was fairly obvious."

"You could have told me," I said. "Jesus. One of you could have bloody told me," I tried to sulk for a while. "So, anyhow, you seem a lot better. Apart from the new teeth and hair, what else have you been up to?"

Carl had been having a great time. As part of his rehabilitation programme, he'd been taken to visit some special needs children, where he was encouraged to pursue his love of taking stuff apart. Carl and the kids would dismantle radios, record players and vacuum cleaners and build spaceships, cars and robots out of all the bits.

"Those kids are brilliant. You should see them. What's a good name for a teacher? I'm thinking of changing my name."

Carl said he wanted to make a fresh start and that included giving himself a new name. He was serious. We talked for a bit about the Goth Cop again, wondering what new pop stars might have left behind unwanted birth names. We decided the pop singers of today all had really dull names that could really only be their real ones.

Carl talked about going to university and becoming a teacher.

"Or a counsellor." He gestured with his eyes towards a nervous looking stick-thin man who appeared to be talking to himself on a plastic seat by the lift. "Do you see that bloke over there?" he whispered.

"What about him?"

"He's a bit mad," Carl said.

"I thought you all were. Isn't that the idea?"

"He's an obsessive compulsive. I was talking to one of the nurses about him. Apparently his symptoms began innocuously enough. Every time he came down the stairs in his house he'd touch the ceiling with his fingertips like a superstitious footballer coming through the tunnel from the dressing room to the pitch. Then he started touching other things for luck as well. The corners of tables and chairs, bathroom and kitchen taps, the tops of shampoo bottles and coffee cups. He felt compelled to touch window frames, floorboards and anything made of wood. Because of that old superstition I suppose.

"Then he found he couldn't go to bed before going through a strict and yet constantly-changing and time-consuming routine. After brushing his teeth at night he'd touch the hot tap and then the cold tap of the bathroom sink and then he'd touch the hot tap again and the cold tap once more and then he'd move on to the bath taps and touch both of those twice. The hot first then the cold and then back to the sink to repeat the routine, always hot then cold. He couldn't go upstairs to his bed until he'd checked and double-checked all the lights were off, and that he'd unplugged any-heat related kitchen appliances like the iron, the kettle and the toaster. Or anything else that he thought might burst into flames of its own free will while he was asleep.

"He had to make sure all the kitchen drawers were flush with each other and that the knives, forks and spoons were where they should be. Knives on the left, forks in the middle, spoons on the right, teaspoons in the little tray at the front of the drawer. He rearranged any shoes that weren't laid out from left to right too. Everything had to be left-right-left-right. From the placing of his shoes to the way he walked in them. The order in which he climbed into his trouser legs and his socks and the way he shaved. Starting on the left side of his face and finishing on the right.

"And he still couldn't go to bed. He had to first turn over any coins that weren't heads up and place them in a pile with the biggest coins at the bottom and the smallest five pence pieces at the top. And then, finally, he could take the long walk upstairs to bed, touching anything wooden along the way.

"Every day there'd be more things to touch. Twice and then twice again, from left to right, hot then cold. He knew that if he didn't obey his compulsion then something awful would happen to him or his family. He missed important work meetings, he missed trains and buses, because he had to stop and touch so many things along the way. He wet himself on the way to the toilet once because it took him so long to get there."

"That's pretty bad," I said.

"It gets worse. Next, he started to pick up pins. See a pin and pick it up – you know the rhyme. He picked up dressmaking pins and drawing pins, safety pins. Dangerous pins. He would have picked up a bowling pin if he came across one. He also picked up anything he saw on the ground with a similar spelling as a pin, like pennies, pens, pencils and peanuts. And he also had to pick up needles and staples, paperclips, nails and screws. Things he counted as part of the wider pin family.

"Then things got really serious. He became obsessed with the number 22. He read in a magazine about how Haiti's tyrannical ruler, Papa Doc, was obsessed by the number and how he believed that voodoo spirits protected him on the 22nd day of every month. That was the only day Papa Doc would leave his presidential palace. When President Kennedy, who Papa Doc had placed a curse upon, was assassinated on the 22nd November he felt his voodoo had been proven to be successful."

Carl nodded in the direction of the nervous stick-thin man.

"What if Papa Doc was right, he thought. So he stopped doing anything or going anywhere on the 22nd day of each month. This left him with only three hundred and forty odd other days a year to get through, which – taking into account national life expectancy, heredity, genetics and whatever – would mean only another ten thousand days or so of living purgatory and disappointment before it would all be over for him. That was ten thousand days too long and he took a load of pills and ended up here."

"Fucking hell," I said.

"I've cured him," Carl said.

"You've cured him?"

"Practically. Once the nurses have passed on my advice, he should be cured. I suggested to the nurses that they get him to have all his belongings put into storage. All his cupboards and drawers, anything made of wood. He should take out all his window frames and replace them with UPVC ones, do the same with all the doors. Get rid of all the wood. Put the whole lot in storage. His bathroom and kitchen taps can be replaced too. With single mixer taps, no left and right, hot and cold anymore. Remove temptation. He'll have nothing to touch." Carl looked pleased with himself, clasping his hands behind his head and swinging his feet up onto a chair.

"What about the twenty two number thing?" I said.

"I can't be expected to do everything. I've got to leave something for all the doctors. Shall we get out of here?"

"I think that would be a good idea," I said. "Shall I distract the guards while you tie some sheets together?"

"You could. But it might be easier if we just walked out. I've been discharged."

While we packed Carl's stuff into carrier bags, he asked me a question.

"If you could put whatever you wanted into storage forever, what would you choose?"

"What, anything?"

"Whatever you want. Animal, vegetable or mineral. Or other."

I folded Carl's get well soon cards into one another, put them in a Tesco bag and thought about his question. "What would you put in?" I said.

"My agliophobia." Carl said.

"Your what?"

"My agliophobia. It's the fear of pain."

"But you tried to cut off your own arm. You pulled out your teeth and hacked your finger off. *Fear of pain, Carl?"*

"It's difficult to explain."

We carried on packing the carriers.

"Can I put the MacDonald's Happy Meal into storage?" I said.

Carl said, "Why?"

"Because it doesn't live up to its name. And also all the videos I've got at home where the central theme revolves around the leading character's neglect of his son or daughter. Symbolised by them missing their baseball game or school play. And then," I said, "I'd need to up the size of my space, because I'd put away all my foibles in a big box along with my idiosyncrasies and weaknesses."

Carl said, "I'd nail a row of coat-hooks to the wall of my storage unit and I'd hang up all my hang-ups."

We carried on like this. I filled up my hypothetical storage space with a lot of the things that I'd learned that I didn't really need to know. I said I'd use the brain space it freed up by finally learning how to drive, or mastering a new language. I'd purge myself of knowing the alphabet backwards and that Bono's real name was Paul Hewson and that Istanbul used to be called Constantinople. I'd make myself forget that the Marquis of Queensbury was cremated in Woking in 1900.

Carl said he no longer had use for knowing that it was only i before e except after c most of the time, and I said I'd gladly rid myself of the burden of carrying around the knowledge that over 2,500 left-handed people are killed each year from using products made for right-handed people. I wouldn't have to feel bad about lending tools to a left-handed customer ever again.

Between us we went on to put a whole lot of other useless rubbish into storage, including knowing that if the Mount Rushmore heads had bodies they'd be nearly five hundred feet tall and that X-rays showed there were three different versions of the Mona Lisa under the visible one. I got rid of the knowledge that the electric chair was invented by a dentist and that a zebra is white with black stripes, not the other way round.

So what if the escalator from Fine Jewellery and Luxury Watches to Lingerie and Nightwear in Harrods was Britain's oldest moving staircase and only one child in twenty are born on the day predicted by the doctor? So what? Who cares if the Hundred Years War lasted 116 years or the human brain is eighty per cent water and ninety eight per cent of the weight of that water is oxygen? We didn't need to know that anymore. The one hundredth piece of surplus knowledge that we threw into storage was that Albert Einstein's last words died with him because the nurse who was with him when he died didn't understand German.

On the way out of the psychiatric hospital we agreed that we would rid ourselves forever of all our disappointments and regrets. We would regret nothing.

"Like Edith Piaf," Carl said. "Regret nothing and celebrate everything."

"Next New Year's Eve, Carl, we should go out on the town. Crack open a bottle of champagne and link arms with all our friends and with complete strangers. Instead of sitting at home alone watching Big Ben on television like we usually do. Rather than bemoaning the end of another year of miserable wasted opportunity we'll celebrate the start of twelve more months of glorious possibility!"

And in the psychiatric hospital's corridor that smelled of Dettol and plastic, using his carrier bags for balance, Carl actually leapt sideways into the air and clicked both his heels together. Anyone watching would have thought he was insane.

I didn't want to send Carl running back for psychiatric help by making him take the 666 bus away from it. The bus would be packed now. It would be like the outside of a nightclub on a Friday at closing time. Passengers would be arguing with the bus driver. No one would have a valid ticket and anybody who did would have stolen it from someone else. There'd be no seats free downstairs and we'd have to go up to the top deck where there'd be a fight. The bus driver would stop the bus and switch off the engine for a stand off with a group of schoolchildren about how the bus would not be moving until they left it.

Instead I dialled the minicab number that was sellotaped to the wall above the same hospital payphone I'd rung Janie on earlier. The cab driver turned out to be another one of my number one fans.

"I didn't recognise you under all that, under the bruising and whatnot," he said. "I am right though aren't I? You are who I think you are aren't… Oh, hang on a minute…"

I watched the cab driver's eyes reflected in his rear view mirror as they moved back and forth between staring at me, the road ahead and the glove box where he was rifling through some old cassette tapes. There was one of those Magic Tree air fresheners hanging from the mirror. It was a pink one. And although it didn't really smell anything like it I could see the word at the foot of the tree was WATERMELON.

"Here it is," he said. "See if you recognise this."

He put a tape into his shitty car stereo and we all waited for the hiss to finish and the music to start. When it did the music sounded like it was playing on an old vinyl record that had been left in front of a window on a sunny day. The tape kept slowing down, the volume was fading in and out and only the left speaker was working.

And it bothered me, even now, all these years after I'd

recorded the song. It bothered me that the cab driver was making us listen to it like this. All that time spent in the studio getting the sound right. Trying to get the perfect balance between the guitars and the vocals. Hours spent turning the snare drum up and then down again until it was in the right place in the mix. Until it was at a volume where the drummer was happy with it and yet it wasn't the only thing you could hear on the record. All that time and money spent agonising over the sound, with the studio engineer tweaking the knobs and faders in tinier and tinier amounts, like he was cracking a safe. Mixing and remixing, tweaking and balancing, shipping the finished recording over to New York to be mastered by *the sweetest ears in the industry*. All that effort, expertise and expense when people can't even be bothered to have both the speakers in their car working.

I rolled down the cab window just enough to poke my head out, like a dog on the motorway on a hot day, the wind blowing in my Elephant Man face while the sound of a younger and higher-pitched me oscillated back and forth in volume from Carl's side of the car. I listened to the song and couldn't remember what the lyrics meant.

The cabbie was talking. Raising his voice above the fluctuating loud bits in the song. I tried to block out the sound of both our voices and listened to the cab's engine and the whoosh of cars and lorries passing by in the opposite direction. We stopped at some traffic lights and a cyclist almost took the cab's wing mirror and my head off as he sped past to jump the red light.

"*Cock face!*" He shouted back at us. He must have been referring to the cab driver. I was Melon Head. The cab driver must have been Cock Face.

The lights changed and we started moving again. We were into the second song on the album now and I hoped it wasn't the start of a box set of old hissy cassettes of my music. It was the same now as it had always been – even all those years when I'd thought of myself as a genius. I'd never really liked the sound of my own voice.

The view from the open cab window was the same view as the one I'd seen from the bus on the way to see Carl. It was on the other side of the road and moving in the opposite direction, but it was the same view nevertheless. The same cereal packet buildings placed at the side of the road by playschool children. Every once in a while the town planner toddlers had introduced a cardboard tube from the inside of a toilet roll to represent a graffiti covered post box, a mobile phone mast or a piss-stained lamppost.

The cab driver called me back into the car with a question. "So what is it you do these days? Still making the old music?"

"Storage," I said. My head still out the window, passing pedestrians must have thought me weird, shouting the word storage at them. I pulled my head back into the car and rolled the window back up. "I'm in storage. Well not me exactly. *I'm* not in storage, but that's what I do for a job."

"I should get some of that," the driver said. "Our house is chock-a-block. Heaving with junk, it is. Sandra, my wife, says where she came from they didn't have a pot to piss in. She reckons that's why there was less rubbish on the streets. Not like here. The streets are a disgrace here. My wife says where she grew up they had nothing so they didn't chuck away what they did have. The roads were all potholed and little more than dirt tracks sometimes, but there wasn't a scrap of litter. I don't suppose they had much of a need for storage space either. What they had they used. No excess baggage. What you might call a utilitarian way of life." I guessed it wasn't the first time he'd used that sentence.

If his wife - what was her name? Sandra? - if Sandra went

back home to wherever it was she came from now she'd probably find it had all changed. The streets would be littered with the same shit as the one her husband was driving us along now.

I went on a tour of East Germany just after the Berlin Wall came down and one thing I noticed was how quickly the billboards and advertising hoardings for Pepsi and Western cigarettes went up as soon as the borders were open. It was as though gangs of men with ladder-topped vans packed with posters and buckets of wallpaper paste had been waiting with their engines running on the West side of the wall since 1961.

If the tour had been a bit longer, maybe after the fizzy drink and fag ads were up I would have seen the storage companies following closely behind. With all their new capitalist possessions the East Germans were going to need somewhere to put them all. No doubt somewhere big and yellow. Die große gelbe speicherfirma.

People will always need space. Space to think. Room to breathe. And somewhere to stash all their crap. All those obsolete television sets and video recorders, record players and radios. Obsolete yet still working. One day all that stuff would no longer be just obsolete. It would become retro and sought after, valuable antiques even. People would need somewhere to keep it all till then. Along with all their unused sports equipment and clothes that don't fit.

All the unwanted Christmas presents, unread coffee table books taking up coffee table space. Coffee tables. The shoe mountains and the homicidal computers. Battery collections, unfinished gravestones, ships made out of matchsticks and all of mine and Carl's insecurities, foibles and phobias.

And like that American storage big Mac and cheese Jack J Renumba once said: London has density. It's a claustrophobic city. I needed to get back to work. London needed me.

Ronan Keating once sang about life being a rollercoaster. Maybe he was right. Sometimes it will be a brand new state of the art, computerised, white-knuckle ride rollercoaster. Full of thrills, laughter and loop the loops. At the end of the ride you'll get a photograph in a cardboard frame with everyone you met and loved in your rollercoaster life freeze framed on film in the middle of a scream of ecstasy and excitement. Afterwards you'll stuff your face with candy floss and toffee apples then go and spend twenty quid and half an hour trying to pick up a stuffed toy that cost two pence to make with a motorized claw.

For others, life will be a different rollercoaster ride. A rollercoaster ride in the pouring rain. A wet rollercoaster ride full of terrified, screaming and crying children, all holding on for dear life wishing it was over. For others, they'll be sat in the front seat with the feel of the crying and terrified children's warm projectile vomit splashing onto the back of their cold necks. Sat in the front seat of a wet, sick-stinking rollercoaster ride that's part of a fun fair that's seen far better days. In a rusty old rollercoaster car that will skid in the rain, tipping up and coming off the wet rails, flying through the salty air and crashing into the beautiful briny, shivery shiny, shit-coloured English Channel.

But still a rollercoaster ride.

So. That's where I am now. Tell your readers. Stick me in your magazine. Slap a big exclamation mark on a bad picture of me if you like. That's where I am now. I'm at the fun fair.

I switched HAL on and wrote a letter.

Dear Mr. Bus Station Man,

As a frequent user of your bus station I have enjoyed the piped classical music but may I suggest, as beautiful a piece of music as The 'O Fortuna' chorus *is, may I suggest it unsuitable for bus waiting in a scary area. If you insist on continuing with this piece of music may I suggest a few additions to your disco, perhaps the* Jaws Theme, The Exorcist *music, which I believe is Mike Oldfield's* Tubular Bells, *and* Somebody's Gonna Get Their Head Kicked In Tonight *by The Rezillos.*

Yours faithfully

An apprehensive passenger

On the way to the post box I met the pornobomber coming in with a fresh box of filth or death.

"How are the boybands?" he asked.

"The boybands?" I said. "Oh, the boybands. I'm afraid the boybands have escaped."

"Escaped?"

"Uh huh. Last night. Just checked the CCTV cameras. Caught it all on tape."

I told him how Ronan Keating's solo career had begun to make him lonely. How he'd fallen out with Louis Walsh and how he wanted to get the Boyz back together. I told him that Ronan had packed himself in a large box much like his old Svengali mates had done back at the football ground, and how he'd had the box delivered here. Then, under cover of night, watched only by the closed circuit television cameras, he emerged from his box. With the keys he'd picked from Louis Walsh's pocket he unlocked the door of the boyband room at the far, far end of the building where the light bulbs have all blown and nobody ever goes.

And Ronan released them all. Bad Boys Inc, 3SL, Code Red and Big Fun, 911, Upside Down, The Backstreet Boys, 98 Degrees, O*town, Human Nature and all the others. He led them all outside, past the recycling bins and on down dogshit alley, fighting their way through the swarm of gnats and away into the night to divide and multiply. To form new bands, go solo, or try their hand at acting or television presenting.

"Yes, I'm afraid Pandora's Box is well and truly open. God only knows what will happen now."

Walking away, I stopped and looked back at the man who was still standing there looking a bit confused, his arms sagging under the weight of his stash of pornography and bombs.

"Just like that old Greek story," I said to him. "The box is empty, there's nothing left. Nothing at all," I carried on walking and then pulled one last Columbo turn and said, "Except hope."

Nothing left but hope. I liked that. I was pleased with myself for having said that. I should write books. Maybe I would. Maybe I'd write a book about a rock star who turns his back on the fame to work in self-storage. I could end it in the way all those films about rock bands end. Have the anti-hero walk onstage at a big concert and strap on a guitar to join in on a song with his old bandmates. The big concert could be at a football ground. He could be wheeled to the stage in a silver flightcase. Tom Paulin would hate it when he reviewed it on BBC2.

Continuing out into the street to post my bus company letter, I found my Richard Briers whistle was back. It was more breath than tune and it hurt my fat cheek but it felt good. Stopping off at the most miserable sweetshop in the world for a stamp I told the man behind the counter that it was okay. Everything was going to be all right.

Leaving the shop, I posted the bus station letter and turned back towards work. I needed to put some new strings on my guitar before Janie got in. And then there was just one other thing I had to do.

ALARM
o—r—s— e odyssey
2001

In case you're left wondering:

Terrorvision are a British rock band formed in 1987 in Bradford. They broke up in 2001 and later reformed. Their biggest hit single was a 1999 Mint Royale remix of the song Tequila. *Their singer Tony was a big hit as a very funny guest on the pop quiz and comedy show* Never Mind The Buzzcocks.

Actress Parminder Nagra appeared in the film Bend It Like Beckham *before going on to play Doctor Neela Rasgotra in the American TV series* ER.

Siegfried and Roy are flamboyantly costumed, spectacular Las Vegas magicians. The world's most famous white tiger vanishers and self proclaimed Masters of The Impossible.

The reason you don't see dried up white dog turds on the streets anymore is because bones have been largely removed from the canine diet. The bones caused a calcium overload and led to the white poo.

The Pet Shop Boys have always been considered to be the most ironic pop group in the world.

ACKNOWLEDGEMENTS

Thanks to Holly, Marc, Neil, Chris, Cerise, Emma and Jacqueline for reading my many rewrites and for encouraging me to continue. Thanks to Tim Connery for his painstaking proof reading work, to Neil Witherow for putting the thing together and also going swimming with me. Thanks to John for his wonderful art and invaluable expert help and for being a dude. Thanks to Camilla Goslett for early encouragement. To Andrew Collins for his constant and unfashionable support. Thanks to Tony Wright. And a big thank you to Jacqueline and Holly for putting up with a wannabe author in the house, as if a wannabe pop star wasn't enough to put up with already.

ABOUT THE AUTHOR

Jim Bob is a London singer and songwriter and author of the critically acclaimed autobiography Goodnight Jim Bob – On the Road With Carter The Unstoppable Sex Machine. His favourite animal is the elephant.

Here he is wearing shades. Like Bono.

ALSO BY THE SAME AUTHOR

Goodnight Jim Bob - On the Road
With Carter The Unstoppable Sex Machine
Published by Cherry Red Books

'Singer Jim Bob's memoirs are a hoot, as if Hunter S. Thompson had gone on the road with Spinal Tap.'
OK MAGAZINE

'If you can't remember the duo, with their pun laden songs about South London, it matters nought; this is a book about an everyband, and should be read by every other band when they aren't watching Spinal Tap.'
MOJO MAGAZINE

'Jim captures the very essence of life on and off the road for the 90s' least likely pop stars. A good dash of Hammer Of The Gods, a healthy glug of Ian Hunter's Diary Of A Rock'n'Roll Star and absolutely no trace of Sting's Broken Music.'
ANDREW COLLINS

'A cracking page-turner from one of the finest song lyricists of the last twenty years. This book deserves to be seen as the 'Fever Pitch' of rock 'n' roll.'
ROBERT NEWMAN

'Jim Bob's prose is as irreverent and frequently as laugh out loud funny as his music, his anecdotes leaving you wondering why on earth anyone would want to be in even a moderately successful band.'
LOGO MAGAZINE

‘Hilariously self aware of Carter's standing in musical history, Mr Bob writes touchingly of the joy he felt on stage for an hour a night - and with an Alan Bennett eye about the 23 hours of tedium that goes with it. Killingly funny about CUSM's brief time at the top, it makes his despair at the slow decline all the more poignant. Laughter, tears and more bad puns than is humanly decent. Cult smash.’
CHANNEL 4

‘Laugh-out-loud bitesize chunks of deranged pop excess mix freely with embarrassed nostalgia. With excellent prose and sophisticated layering, Jim Bob has written a better book than one would reasonably expect, though it should've been obvious from a decade of bittersweet lyrics. And if this hilarious account does anything, it should remind people that actually, during the grunge years, we did ok. A finely printed calling card for the good life on the road.’
DROWNED IN SOUND

‘Jim Bob's sprawling biography/travelogue is just as irritating and petulant and inspirational as the band it portrays, and this book is a sometimes bitter sweet, sometimes smug, always evocative look at a time that I, for one, would rather forget.’
PLAN B MAGAZINE

‘An irreverent peek into the music world which is laugh out loud funny.’
SOUTH LONDON PRESS

‘A tissue of lies.’
FRUITBAT